"I kissed you. And you liked it!"

She took a sharp intake of breath, swallowing hard. He was right; she had liked it....

"I think your ego may be getting in the way again, Jarrett," Abbie told him. "You just can't seem to accept that every female you meet isn't going to fall willingly into your arms! I'll admit I was curious for a while, but—despite what you may have thought— my husband was a more-than-capable lover. He knew exactly how to please a woman." Her gaze was coolly steady on Jarrett's now angry face. "No other man could ever take his place in my life."

"I don't want to take his place!" Jarrett visibly recoiled. "You already know my views on marriage—"

"And you already know mine on affairs...."

Jarrett, Jonathan and Jordan
are

Some men are *meant* to marry!

Meet three brothers: Jarrett is the eldest—Hunter by name, hunter by nature. Jonathan's in the middle and a real charmer; there's never been a woman whom he wanted and couldn't have. Jordan is the youngest and he's devilishly attractive. But he's determined never to succumb to emotional commitment.

These bachelor brothers appear to have it all— looks, wealth, power.... But what about love? That's where Abbie, Gaye and Stazy come in. As Jarrett, Jonathan and Jordan are about to discover—wanting a woman is one thing, winning her heart is quite another....

Look out for Jonathan's story next month!

CAROLE MORTIMER

To Woo a Wife

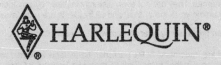

TORONTO • NEW YORK • LONDON
AMSTERDAM • PARIS • SYDNEY • HAMBURG
STOCKHOLM • ATHENS • TOKYO • MILAN • MADRID
PRAGUE • WARSAW • BUDAPEST • AUCKLAND

For Peter

ISBN 0-373-12039-7

TO WOO A WIFE

First North American Publication 1999.

Look us up on-line at: http://www.romance.net

Printed in U.S.A.

CHAPTER ONE

'It isn't that I don't appreciate the suggestion that I join you all for dinner, Stephen,' the man drawled in a bored voice. 'It's just that making up a foursome isn't something I've made a habit of; I've inevitably found that any woman deliberately out on her own for the evening is either on the hunt for a rich man—or, even worse, she's a paper-bag job!'

The woman dismissed as either 'on the hunt for a rich man—or even worse…a paper-bag job' had entered the hotel lounge and bar seconds ago, and had been in the process of locating her hosts for the evening—her friend Alison and her new husband Stephen—when she had unwittingly overheard the man's insulting remark.

She had found Alison and Stephen—and they weren't alone. Not that Abbie could actually see them, or they her, hidden behind the huge plant that stood majestically in the plush room. And, in view of what the man had just said, perhaps it was as well!

'I think that's a bit strong, Jarrett,' Alison protested indignantly. ''These days, women can go anywhere, and do anything they want to do. And we don't need a man to do it with!'

Well, at least Abbie knew his name now. Jarrett… It meant nothing to her.

'Do these ''go-anywhere'' women get married?' the man called Jarrett taunted pointedly.

'They have the right to choose that option if they wish to—as I did,' Alison returned heatedly. 'I'm just point-

ing out that we don't need a man for our very existence,
as our grandmothers did, and possibly our mothers too.
We have careers now, earn our own money, and therefore marriage isn't the necessity it once was—'

Stephen's husky laugh interrupted her. 'I have a feeling you're being deliberately wound up, my love.'

The other man laughed too. 'Guilty, I'm afraid. I'm
sorry, Alison, it really isn't fair of me when you're still
on your honeymoon. I think it's great that the two of
you decided to get married. I'm only sorry I missed the
wedding. I find it incredible that I've bumped into the
two of you like this. I had no idea you were coming to
Canada skiing.'

Abbie had missed the wedding too, which was why,
after numerous protests that she hadn't wanted to inter-
rupt their honeymoon, she had accepted the couple's invitation to join them this evening. But it was obvious
from this man Jarrett's comments that his meeting with
the newly-weds was purely coincidental.

If Abbie had thought it was anything else, that she
was possibly being set up with this man by well-meaning
friends, then she would have turned around and left the
hotel without even making her presence here known,
would simply have telephoned her apologies. But she
didn't really think that was the case; Alison was well
aware of her feelings towards relationships. They simply
didn't exist as far as Abbie was concerned.

Although she had to admit Jarrett's initial remark had
stung, making her look critically at herself in one of the
mirrors that lined the bar walls. As tall as a model, her
legs were long and shapely; she was wearing a black
sheath of a dress that moulded her figure, its length a
couple of inches short of her knees. But over the stylish
dress she had put on a thin silk jacket the same violet-

blue colour of her eyes, its loose style detracting from the clinging material of her dress. Her long dark hair was pulled back in a neat chignon, her make-up subtly delicate.

She tried to see herself through the man Jarrett's eyes, and decided he would think her cool and aloof, not quite a 'paper-bag job', but certainly not vibrantly beautiful either!

'Nevertheless,' Jarrett continued lightly, 'I really do have to turn down your invitation to join you all. Your friend may not mind playing gooseberry, Alison, but I certainly do!'

Abbie felt the heat in her cheeks at what she was sure was a rebuke aimed at her in her absence. But she had been intensely reluctant too when Alison had asked her to join herself and Stephen this evening, conscious that the couple were still on their honeymoon. But Alison had completely pooh-poohed the idea of Abbie intruding, reminding her she and Stephen had lived together for a year before their wedding two weeks ago, and that they certainly weren't in the first romantic flush of togetherness!

Abbie moved as quietly away from the trio and from behind the huge plant as she had approached them, going out to the powder-room in the lobby. Once there she removed her jacket, replenished her make-up but applied it more deeply this time, and made a final alteration to her hair as she deftly removed all the pins that held it so neatly in place. The result was a wild tumble of black gypsy-like strands almost down to her waist, the flowing darkness highlighting her high cheekbones, the clear beauty of her eyes, and the pouting fullness of her mouth.

A paper-bag job—huh!

She left the jacket in the cloakroom with the warm outer coat she had deposited there earlier, crossing the reception area with long, easy strides, aware of the male interest that followed her progress, but not acknowledging it by so much as a flick of her long black hair, the light of challenge sparkling in her violet-blue eyes.

That male reaction to her looks spoke for itself; she wasn't 'on the hunt for a rich man', either, the diamonds that sparkled in her earlobes and wrist giving testament to that. She couldn't help wondering, a little gleefully, she admitted, exactly what Jarrett was going to make of her!

She didn't pause inside the bar this time but walked straight over to the table where she knew Alison and Stephen sat with the other man. She smiled widely at her friend as Alison looked up and saw her approach.

'Abbie!' Alison stood up to hug her warmly. 'You look wonderful!' she stood back to say admiringly—if slightly surprised too. Alison had been at the forefront of the friends who had gently chided her during the last couple of years for playing down the looks that had once engendered the interest of some of the most powerful men in the world. To no avail.

'You certainly do.' Stephen stood up to kiss her lightly on the cheek.

The newly-weds made an attractive couple, Alison a tall redhead, Stephen tall and blond. Abbie had known the two of them for years, had always been able to relax and be herself in their company. Except tonight they weren't alone...

She turned coolly to look at the man with the deeply male voice, the man she knew only as Jarrett, feeling the equivalent of a mild electric shock as she saw him for the first time. He was one of those men you would never forget when you had met him: devilishly attractive!

Possibly ten years older than her own twenty-seven, he had lines of experience on that handsome face to go with his maturity. And it was probably those lines, and the cynical light in his assessing amber eyes as he returned her gaze, that saved him from being just too good-looking.

As he politely stood up, Abbie could see he was tall and powerfully built, with not an ounce of superfluous flesh on the lean length of his body that was clothed in a navy blue jacket, pale grey shirt and grey trousers. His dark hair was slightly overlong, curling attractively as it met the collar of his jacket, his face perfectly sculptured, jaw square and determined below a mockingly smiling mouth. But it was his eyes that dominated, that deep gleaming amber one of the most unusual colours Abbie had ever seen. Like the eyes of a tiger…

'Abbie, this is a friend of mine from London.' Stephen stepped in to introduce the two of them. 'Jarrett Hunter.'

Hunter… It suited him, Abbie decided ruefully. 'And I'm Abbie,' she put in smoothly, holding out a long, slender, completely ringless hand, her nails kept short and lacquerless.

He reached out and took her hand in his, his own warm but firm to the touch, his grip neither too tight nor too limp; Daniel had always said you could tell a lot about a man from his handshake. If that were to be believed, this man was neither remote nor overly friendly!

'Just Abbie?' he murmured, that golden gaze blazing on the smooth perfection of her face.

'Just Abbie.' She easily forestalled Stephen as he would have spoken.

'It's what she was known as during our years on the

catwalk together.' Alison spoke lightly as they all resumed their seats, Abbie now occupying a chair to the
other woman's left, with Jarrett Hunter opposite her.

He turned to Abbie with renewed interest, his male
assessment of her feminine attributes made swiftly and
easily. He relaxed back in his own armchair. ''So you're
a model, too,' he murmured appreciatively.

'I was,' she answered quietly, ordering a sparkling
mineral water when a waiter approached her.

Amber eyes widened interestedly. 'But not any more?'

'No, not any more,' she told him before turning back
to the newly married couple, aware as she did so that
Jarrett Hunter was still watching her with narrowed eyes.
She guessed, with a certain amount of amusement at his
expense, that he was having trouble categorising her.
Like Alison, as a model, she had been assessed and pro-
cessed and put into the appropriate box. Since she was
no longer a model but obviously self-assured and mod-
erately wealthy at least, he was obviously wondering exactly what she was now. She didn't think he had a hope
of guessing!

'I can't tell you how pleased we are to see you here,
Abbie.' Alison leant forward to clasp her arm. 'We don't
see half enough of you these days,' she added with disappointment.

Abbie shrugged, aware that, for all he appeared perfectly relaxed and uninterested as he sat back in his
chair, Jarrett Hunter was actually listening intently to
every word spoken. Obviously he was a man who didn't
like mysteries—and she was fast becoming one to him!

'I don't know where the time goes,' she answered
regretfully. 'One day I'm in London, the next in Hong
Kong, and today I'm in Canada!'

'You enjoy travelling, Abbie?' Jarrett Hunter was regarding her rather scornfully now, perhaps envisaging her as a social butterfly with a certain amount of contempt.

Abbie coolly returned his scathing glance. 'Not particularly, Mr Hunter,' she drawled dismissively.

Puzzlement flickered in those amber depths as he frowned slightly. 'Then why——?'

'I believe our table is ready.' Stephen smoothly cut in on their conversation as the waiter approached their table again, his blue eyes widely innocent as Jarrett turned to him to protest. 'I know you said earlier that you were busy this evening, Jarrett, but are you sure you won't join us?' he added.

Abbie's mouth quirked slightly with amusement as she looked admiringly at her friend's new husband; Stephen could almost be aware that she had overheard Jarrett Hunter's stinging remarks earlier at her expense! Or maybe he was just finding his friend's male reaction to her, after his earlier scathing comments about single women, a cause for amusement himself...! Whatever, Stephen was enjoying this situation immensely!

'I——'

'Please don't think of changing your arrangements on my account.' Abbie gave Jarrett Hunter a bright, vacuous smile as they all stood up. 'Gone are the days, I can assure you, when we women needed a male escort to be able to go out to dinner. Thank goodness'!' she added with feeling.

Alison gave her a sharp, questioning look before glancing towards the entrance to the bar, obviously taking in the presence of the large, concealing plant that stood near their seats, a knowing look in her eyes now as she met Abbie's innocent gaze.

Jarrett Hunter was looking at her with narrowed eyes

too, but for a completely different reason. He was still trying to fit her into a particular niche—and failing utterly! 'I don't actually have any other arrangements for dinner this evening,' he finally said slowly. 'I just didn't want to intrude…'

'How kind of you,' Abbie said. 'Alison and I have so much news to catch up on.'

'…on Alison and Stephen's honeymoon,' Jarrett Hunter finished softly, challenge in those golden eyes now.

He had very capably turned the tables on her, trying—and succeeding!—in putting her in a defensive position. But not an irretrievable one—

'Alison and I have been married almost two weeks; we go home the day after tomorrow—the honeymoon is over!' Stephen very neatly came to her rescue.

Alison tucked her arm possessively through the crook of his. 'Only the social part,' she warned.

'Take a tip from me, Jarrett,' Stephen told his friend with an affected groan. 'Never marry a younger woman!'

Abbie and Alison were both twenty-seven, whereas the two men were probably in their late thirties, though considering they looked athletically fit, their bodies lithe and firm, Stephen's last remark had to be a joke. And it was one that Abbie and Alison both responded to.

Not so Jarrett Hunter. 'I never intend marrying at all,' he drawled arrogantly.

Abbie looked at him with new interest; so the two of them had something in common, after all. She had no intention of ever being married, either. But she had her own reasons for that decision. She wondered what Jarrett Hunter's were…

'Why settle for one delicious dessert?' He scornfully

supplied the answer to her question, even as she thought it. 'When I have a liking for so many?' he added.

Abbie was beginning actively to dislike him—and his sweeping statements!

'But I happen to know I like strawberry trifle best,' Stephen told the other man, with an affectionate grin at Alison's red hair.

'Maybe you do like it best,' Jarrett Hunter accepted in a bored voice. 'But a constant diet of it could become—tedious.'

'You have a sweet tooth, Mr Hunter?' Abbie put in swiftly as she saw Alison was about to explode indignantly at the insult he had just delivered to her two-week-old marriage with his double-edged conversation. Not surprisingly, in the circumstances!

Jarrett turned to her with cool golden eyes. 'No more than the next man—Abbie,' he returned.

She could see by looking at him that he was a virile man, that he had probably had more than his fair share of women attracted to his arrogant attractiveness. But, considering Alison and Stephen were on their honeymoon, his remark was highly inflammatory.

'Really?' Abbie replied consideringly. 'I don't have a sweet tooth at all, so I don't have that particular problem.' She drew his remarks back to her, and away from the much more volatile Alison; her friend's red hair was indicative of her fiery nature, and if Jarrett Hunter wasn't careful he was going to end up floored by Alison's heated remarks. And that would be a pity, when she and Stephen had obviously enjoyed their honeymoon so far.

That golden gaze travelled the length of her shapely legs, over the sensuous curves of her body so lovingly outlined by the fitted black dress, up to the beauty of her face, surrounded by a dark tumble of long hair. 'You surprise me, Abbie,' he murmured dryly.

'Do I?' Violet-blue eyes steadily met gold.

'Well, perhaps not,' he replied with slow deliberation. 'I've always thought that chocolate éclairs look appetising, until you bite into them and find there's no substance.' He gave a grimace, his gaze still holding hers.

Abbie could feel the angry colour rising in her cheeks even as she heard Alison gasp at the force of his remark. He was being deliberately insulting. But then, so was she. In fact, she had probably goaded him into this exchange, still stung by those earlier comments of his that she'd overheard.

'Thank goodness I save myself the disappointment,' she dismissed lightly. 'Dinner, people,' she announced pointedly.

'Jarrett?' Stephen prompted, grinning as he had enjoyed the exchange.

That golden gaze once more ran the length of Abbie's slenderly alluring body, pausing briefly on the curve of her hips and breasts, before once again pausing on the beauty of her face. 'As long as Abbie doesn't mind,' he murmured challengingly. 'After all, I am being rather forced on her for the evening,' he added smoothly.

This was the very last thing she wanted, an evening spent in Jarrett's abrasive company not something she would deliberately wish on herself. And he knew it too, which was probably the reason why he had made the challenge in the first place.

'You will be Alison and Stephen's guest, not mine,' she returned distantly.

Dark brows rose over those golden eyes. 'In that case—I accept the invitation.'

She had known that he would, known that somehow

he couldn't resist the opportunity of finding out more about her. He no more found her a chocolate éclair without substance than he did a 'paper-bag job'!

'You overheard him earlier, didn't you?' Alison spoke softly at Abbie's side as the two women preceded the men into the hotel restaurant, her arm draped loosely through the crook of Abbie's. 'You came into the bar and heard what he was saying about—'

'Who on earth is he?' Abbie hissed indignantly. 'I've never met such an arrogant, overbearing, pompous, self-opinionated—'

'You did overhear him.' Alison giggled gleefully. 'Isn't he just unbelievable?' She glanced back briefly to where the two men strolled along behind them chatting idly together.

'The man is a dinosaur!' Abbie returned disgustedly, shaking her head, aware of his golden eyes on her now, and the gentle sway of her hips, as she walked. Her years on the catwalk had given her the confidence not even to falter.

'Who doesn't believe in marriage,' her friend acknowledged happily. 'The two of you could be kindred spirits!'

'Don't be ridiculous, Alison,' Abbie protested impatiently. 'You heard the man; he likes a little taste of every dessert there is going, whereas I—'

'Don't have a sweet tooth,' Alison finished with another giggle. 'What a marvellous conversation that was,' she added admiringly.

Abbie frowned at her friend. 'You didn't seem to find it so funny when he was being so disparaging about Stephen's preference for strawberry trifle!'

Alison grinned. 'So, I've never met a misogynist before—'

'He isn't a woman-hater, Alison; he devours them!' Abbie corrected her disgustedly. 'And the ones he finds unpalatable he spits out again!'

Alison gave the two men another glance. 'If I weren't so in love with Stephen I might have a go at proving him wrong!'

'You and several hundred other women,' Abbie replied scathingly. 'It's his ploy, Alison. It's the way he gets a taste of every dessert; every woman thinks she'll be his favourite flavour—and not just of the month!'

'We're doing it too now.' Her friend laughed softly. 'But you have to admit, he isn't a man any woman could just ignore.'

Not even her, Abbie inwardly acknowledged. But outwardly she would never admit such a thing. 'You do realise I'm going to choose the most expensive thing on the menu as retribution, don't you?' she said dryly, deeply annoyed with herself for even being aware of Jarrett Hunter.

'That's okay,' her friend said easily. 'We wouldn't be here at all if you hadn't given us this wonderful honeymoon as our wedding present, so the least we can do is take you out to dinner as a way of saying thank you.'

But it was a thank-you Abbie had tried hard to get out of earlier today. It was purely coincidence that she happened to be in Canada at the same time as them.

'I don't need a thank-you, Alison—'

'I believe we are at our table, ladies.' Jarrett Hunter smoothly cut in on their conversation, he and Stephen pulling back the two chairs at the round table to enable them to sit down, a fourth place having been laid for Jarrett.

As she'd expected from the shape of the table, Abbie had Stephen seated on one side of her, and Jarrett on the other, and lucky Alison had exactly the same arrangement. What a wonderful evening this was going to be!

Abbie had to admit that Alison and Stephen did appear to be enjoying themselves, Stephen even sending Abbie a conspiratorial wink over the top of the menu he was supposed to be looking at.

The menus they were all looking at. Except Abbie couldn't seem to concentrate on hers, because she was so very conscious of the hard, arrogant man seated to her left.

Who was Jarrett Hunter? What was he doing here? He didn't seem the sort of man who would take a holiday on his own, but who would probably be quite happy to put up with the tedium of a constant diet of a single dessert for a couple of weeks or so. It had to be better, from his point of view, than being without a dessert at all!

Yet he appeared to be alone here, otherwise he would surely have been with his partner this evening. So what was he doing here alone in a Canadian skiing resort in the middle of January? Somehow, glancing surreptitiously at his hard, unyielding face, with those enigmatic golden eyes, Abbie didn't think he was about to enlighten them on that particular subject.

'What takes your fancy, Abbie?'

She blinked at the sound of his husky voice, focusing with effort on the ruggedly handsome face dominated by those tiger-like eyes. She knew she hadn't imagined the slightly suggestive tone of his voice, could see the mockery in those unblinking eyes as he met her gaze.

She closed the menu decisively. 'A green salad, followed by grilled salmon.'

He quirked dark brows. 'I thought you said you were no longer a model?'

'I'm not,' she responded. 'But old habits die hard,' she explained, giving him a considering look. 'Let me guess what you're going to order…' She made a mental inventory of the menu she had just perused. 'Oysters followed by a T-bone steak. Rare!' She quirked her own brows questioningly in return.

'You're right about the steak,' he nodded. 'However, I prefer it to be cooked medium-rare. As for the oysters…!' He grimaced. 'I'm allergic to all shellfish.'

'Really?' Alison interjected interestedly. 'What happens if you eat it?'

'Ignore my little ghoul, Jarrett,' Stephen advised with a rueful shake of his head at his wife. 'We really don't need to know what happens.'

'You're so squeamish, Stephen,' Alison teased affectionately. 'He almost has to be hospitalised if he cuts himself shaving!' she confided to Abbie and Jarrett.

'Not the ideal person to be your birthing-partner when the time comes,' Jarrett acknowledged.

'Birthing-partner…?' Alison looked puzzled. 'But— I'm not pregnant, Jarrett!' Indignation deepened her voice. 'What on earth made you think that I am?' she demanded as she glared at him, quite put out by the suggestion.

Abbie looked at Jarrett too, amazed to see that he actually looked uncomfortable at the erroneous assumption he had made. And so he should be; cynicism was one thing, this was something else!

'I'm sorry.' Jarrett's apology encompassed Stephen too. 'I just assumed—wrongly, as it turns out,' he acknowledged self-derisively. 'I couldn't think of any other reason why the two of you had— I—'

'Shut up, Jarrett, there's a good chap,' Stephen advised good-naturedly, squeezing Alison's hand reassuringly. 'I merely asked Alison to marry me because I love her, and—'

'She merely accepted because she loves you,' Abbie concluded lightly. 'The best possible reason for getting married!' She shot Jarrett Hunter a censorious frown. Really, the man wasn't safe to be let out on his own; it was a wonder to her he had any friends left to insult! Admittedly, she had been a little surprised herself by Alison and Stephen's decision to get married after all this time, but she certainly hadn't made the outrageous assumption about it that Jarrett Hunter obviously had!

'The best,' Jarrett agreed, shooting Abbie a grateful look for her timely intervention. 'And, to answer your earlier question, Alison, when I eat shellfish, my throat swells up and I can't breathe.'

Abbie's mouth quirked into a smile she couldn't contain. 'Feel like ordering a dozen oysters for him, Alison?' she taunted mischievously.

'Two dozen!' Alison joined in the joke, visibly relaxing as she too began to smile.

'Oh, let's not be too cruel,' Stephen added. 'A dozen and a half should do it!'

'Okay, okay!' Jarrett held up his hands in defeat, grinning ruefully. 'I've apologised for—well, I've apologised,' he amended as Abbie frowned warningly. 'Let's order our meal—minus oysters for me—and I promise to try and keep my cynicism to myself for the rest of the evening!'

Rather a rash promise for him to have made, Abbie thought as they gave the waiter their orders, considering almost every comment Jarrett made was grounded in that cynicism! Although it could be interesting watching him try to keep his promise!

'Thanks for your help just then.' Jarrett leant slightly

towards her to murmur quietly, the newly-weds talking softly to each other now.

Abbie looked at him with cool violet-blue eyes. 'I didn't do it to help you,' she returned as softly. 'You obviously have no idea that Alison had a miscarriage six months ago, that the two of them were absolutely devastated by the loss. And that their wedding two weeks ago had absolutely nothing to do with that; why should it?'

Jarrett looked pale, glancing at the other couple, obviously relieved to see them laughing together. 'You're right, I had no idea...'

'Perhaps a curb on your cynicism for the evening wouldn't be such a bad idea...?' she prompted distantly, not feeling that she had betrayed any confidences by talking of the baby Alison and Stephen had lost; it had been no secret, and with this man's penchant for saying the wrong thing at the wrong time he could do more damage by not being aware of the miscarriage. 'A modification of your misogynistic views?'

He grimaced. 'I've said I'll try.'

He would do a lot more than try, if he didn't want to receive a well-aimed kick under the table from the high heel of one of her shoes!

'I suggest we all begin again, Mr Hunter,' she murmured pointedly.

'Jarrett,' he put in smoothly.

Too smoothly. When she suggested they start again, she didn't mean on a different footing; she still didn't have a sweet tooth! 'Mr Hunter,' she repeated firmly. 'Wake up, you two,' she teased the honeymooners as they gazed into each other's eyes. 'Jarrett is about to tell us all exactly what he's doing in Canada.'

'I am?' he said.

He hadn't moved in his chair, still appeared perfectly relaxed, and yet Abbie sensed there was a sudden tension in him. She wondered why...

'You are,' Abbie confirmed lightly, though there was challenge in the cool blue of her eyes as she calmly met his.

His steely gaze never left Abbie's face as he calmly responded, 'There's no mystery attached to my visit; I'm here to meet someone.'

'Ah-hah.' Stephen pounced interestedly. 'Is she a *crème caramel* or an ice-cream sundae?'

'You're really getting into this, aren't you, darling?' Alison said indulgently.

'Definitely the latter,' Jarrett answered with a meaningful look. 'And it isn't what you're thinking at all, Stephen. This meeting is strictly business.'

'But does the lady in question know that?' his friend asked.

'The "lady" isn't even aware we're going to meet,' Jarrett drawled.

'This gets more and more intriguing.' Alison sat forward. 'Who is she?'

'You're in trouble now, Jarrett,' Stephen warned. 'Alison won't give up until she knows the whole story!'

'There is no story,' Jarrett assured them dryly. 'I told you, I've never met the woman. All I know is that my sources tell me she's as cold as that ice-cream sundae you mentioned, Stephen,' he added hardly.

'Was that a deliberate pun, or purely coincidence?' Stephen grinned. 'Sauces. Ice cream,' he explained pointedly.

Jarrett raised dark brows mockingly. 'I think married life is clearly affecting your brain, Stephen—or else it's all this snow,' he amended with an apologetic glance in

Abbie's direction for his lapse into cynicism. 'You know damn well what I meant just now about sources!' he bit out impatiently. 'I've been hunting down a meeting with this woman for months—'

'That has to be a first!' Stephen taunted, tongue-in-cheek.

Jarrett shook his head, his expression pained. 'I'd forgotten just how damned annoying you could be!' He shook his head.

'Oh, he can be much more annoying than this,' Alison assured him guilelessly.

Jarrett shot her an impatient look too, turning to Abbie. 'Do you suppose it's catching?' he muttered irritably.

'Probably,' she returned, enjoying his discomfort, but also intrigued by the conversation, in spite of herself. 'But don't get too worried; you haven't been around them long enough for the effect to be lasting!'

He raised those golden eyes heavenwards. 'Let's hope you haven't either!'

'You don't get out of this that easily, Jarrett,' Alison went on. 'We all want to know exactly who this elusive woman is, and why you want to meet her.'

Alison was taking this joke a little too far, Abbie thought as she picked up her wine glass and took a sip, although she did have a problem herself imagining any woman piquing this man's interest enough for him to continue the pursuit for months; after all, desserts were perishable, they all had a sell-by date—even ice cream!

Perhaps it was catching, after all...!

Jarrett relaxed back in his chair. 'Her name is Sabina Sutherland,' he announced. 'She's Daniel Sutherland's widow. And I have it on good authority that she's here skiing with her daughter— What the hell...?' He gasped as Abbie choked on the wine she had been drinking, leaning forward to tap her gently on the back. 'Come on, Abbie,' he chided as she mopped at the tears on her cheeks with a tissue hastily supplied by Alison. 'I wasn't suggesting doing anything indecent with either the mother or the daughter!'

Even if he had been, he would be out of luck—because she was Sabina Sutherland, and her daughter, Charlie, was only four years old!

CHAPTER TWO

JARRETT watched with narrowed eyes as Alison and
Abbie left the table, ostensibly so that Abbie could re-
store her make-up after her choking fit. But as far as
Jarrett was concerned you couldn't improve on perfection, and Abbie was the most beautiful woman he had
seen in a decade!

He had felt as if someone had kicked him in the solar
plexus when she'd walked into the bar earlier, had found
himself openly staring at her as she moved gracefully
across the room towards them and he had realised this
was the friend of Alison's who was joining them for
dinner. Her face was absolute perfection, her skin clear
and delicate, her nose beautifully sculptured; her face
was dominated by eyes of violet-blue and a deeply
sensual mouth, the lips full and inviting. As for her
hair—! It reached almost down to her waist in a glorious
cascade of midnight. And her body—

He had better stop right there, could already feel the
stirring of desire in his own body just at the thought of
Abbie's!

He turned to Stephen, his mouth twisting wryly at the
way the other man was watching him. 'Stop looking so
damned pleased with yourself,' he mumbled.

Stephen openly smirked. 'I was merely wondering
what you thought of the "paper-bag job" now.'

'Very funny!' Jarrett didn't appreciate being reminded
of his earlier disparaging remarks. 'Who the hell is she,
Stephen?'

The two men had been friends since their schooldays, and although they often didn't see each other for months at a time, for years on one occasion, the easy friendship continued between them.

Stephen shrugged. 'We've already told you, she's a friend of Alison's from their modelling days together.'

Jarrett shook his head. 'If that woman had ever graced the catwalk, then she would have taken the world by storm!' he said with certainty. Abbie carried herself with a natural grace, would look good in anything—or nothing!

God, he was off again; he wouldn't be able to stand up when the ladies returned to the table if this carried on! He couldn't remember reacting this strongly physically to a woman, just on sight, since his teenage years, and that was twenty years ago.

'But she did, Jarrett,' his friend assured him mockingly. 'For two years she was the most sought-after model in Europe. You probably weren't aware of it because you were busy making your millions in Australia!'

'The last I heard, Australia was still part of the world,' he said dryly.

'It's not the location that's relevant, Jarrett,' Stephen said softly.

No, making his fortune had been his driving force for the last twenty years, the people he had associated with picked out for their own influences, or otherwise, in the business world he mixed in. Models—even ones as beautiful as Abbie!—hadn't been of any interest to him whatsoever. Hadn't been... Because he was certainly interested in Abbie now.

'What happened to her after those two years of acclaim?' he probed softly, eyes narrowed thoughtfully.

'She gave up modelling,' Stephen supplied unhelpfully.

Most unhelpfully, as far as Jarrett was concerned. He hadn't been this interested in a woman in years, and the fact that she seemed so damned elusive— A sudden thought struck him. 'She isn't married, is she, Stephen?' he grated harshly. It would be just his luck if she were; married women were definitely a no-no for him.

His own mother's alley-cat behaviour, and the pain it had caused his father, had made him decide long ago that he would never interfere in another couple's relationship. His parents' turbulent marriage was also the reason he had decided he would never fall in love, never marry. If any man tried to intrude on his marriage, he knew he wouldn't react as mildly as his father had done all those years, that he—

What the hell was he doing even thinking about marriage? It was complete anathema to him, as evidenced by his earlier conversation about desserts, and the attraction of each of them.

He recalled with pleasure how Abbie had answered all of his derisive comments with a jibe of her own. Abbie...! Damn it, he was doing it again. If only she weren't so damned intriguing...!

'Would it bother you if she were married?' Stephen answered his question, his expression deliberately bland.

'Not at all,' Jarrett snapped, impatient with himself for dropping his guard enough to let Stephen know how interesting he found the enigmatic Abbie; he should have remembered earlier what a damned nuisance Stephen could be when he got an idea in his head. And the last thing Jarrett needed at the moment was a matchmaking Stephen! 'Just because you're in the throes of newly married bliss at the moment,' he scorned, 'doesn't mean the rest of us have to join you!'

Stephen chuckled at Jarrett's aggression, not fooled for a moment, turning slightly in his chair to look across the restaurant. 'Ah, here come the ladies now,' he said admiringly. 'Don't they make a striking couple? And for the record, Jarrett,' he leant forward to murmur softly when he received no response from the other man, 'Abbie isn't married!'

'I told you, it doesn't—' Jarrett broke off his angry retort as the women reached their table, his frown turning to a scowl as he stood up and noticed a man, seated alone a couple of tables away, who couldn't seem to take his eyes off Abbie.

Damn it, the woman drew admiring male looks like a magnet! Any man stupid enough to become involved with her would need a chain attached to her ankle to make sure she didn't— God, he was doing it again; he had no intention of becoming involved with her, so why should he give a damn about any other idiot who did?

'Excellent timing,' Stephen told the two ladies as they all sat down and their first course was served to them.

Jarrett took one look across the table at Abbie, and as quickly looked away again. God, no woman should have a mouth as sensuous as hers! And the peach lipgloss she had applied to those pouting lips only made him want to kiss her all the more.

And he did want to kiss her!

In fact, he wanted to do a lot more than kiss her...! Thank goodness he had been able to hold the white linen napkin in front of him when he stood up while the two women resumed their seats, otherwise the whole restaurant would have been aware of the complete betrayal of

his body. He was behaving like a schoolboy with his
first crush, damn it!

The man seated two tables away, although giving the
impression of eating his own meal, was still watching
Abbie, surreptitiously. And Jarrett, again like a schoolboy, he acknowledged angrily, wanted to punch him on
the nose for just daring to look at her!

'Are the ribs not to your liking, Jarrett?'

He looked at Abbie with completely blank eyes; even
the husky tone to her voice was faintly erotic. Damn it,
no woman should be this sensually beautiful. 'What?'
he rasped aggressively.

The slight widening of violet-blue eyes was the only
visible indication she gave of recognising his manner. 'I
merely wondered if there was something wrong with
your food; you don't appear to be eating it,' she pointed
out lightly.

He looked down at the untouched starter in front of
him, across at the other three half-eaten plates of food
on the table, forcing himself to relax, inwardly chastising
himself for his lapse. The sooner he got this meal over
with, the sooner he would be able to get away. From
Abbie.

'I'm sure the ribs are going to be excellent,' he answered. 'After all, this is a Sutherland Hotel, isn't it?'
he added derisively. 'Although,' he continued, 'it isn't
much of a recommendation for the place when the part-
owner doesn't even stay in her own hotels!' He bit into
his food, and, as he had already surmised, the ribs were
mouth-wateringly delicious.

Sutherland Hotels were known worldwide for their
welcoming service and excellent restaurants; everything
about this hotel spoke of its exclusivity, from the reception to the beautifully furnished suites of rooms. But the

woman who dominated the boardroom, Daniel Sutherland's widow, never stayed in them...

According to Daniel Sutherland's daughter Cathy, the eldest of two children from his first marriage, Sabina had been the daughter of one of her father's employees. On her marriage to Daniel Sutherland, she'd very quickly learnt the advantages of having such a wealthy husband. Since his death two years ago, she'd never demeaned herself enough to stay in one of the family hotels, always finding private accommodation close by—on a grand scale!—when she was on one of her regular visits as guardian of the major shareholder in the family business. Sabina's young daughter Charlotte was the real Sutherland heir; Sabina was merely a caretaker until her child achieved the age of twenty-one. But until that time the woman obviously intended to milk the situation for all it was worth!

It was all too easy to see why Cathy, and her younger brother Danny, resented the hold their stepmother had on their inheritance through her own daughter's shares in the company. Daniel Sutherland must have been totally besotted with his second wife to have left his will in the way that he had—

'You're talking of Sabina Sutherland?' Abbie prompted coolly.

'Who else?' he scorned. 'She's staying in a private ski-lodge somewhere up the mountain—'

'And how do you know that?' She looked at him frowningly.

He shrugged. 'I asked around.'

Violet-blue eyes widened. 'And someone here, at the hotel, told you where she was staying?'

'Not here, Abbie.' He gave a smile. 'I'm sure giving out that sort of information about their employer is more than their job is worth! No, I asked around, discreetly, in London, before coming out here to Whistler.'

He had suffered several boring evenings listening to Cathy Sutherland's bitterness about her stepmother, withstanding her more than obvious attempts to deepen their relationship to physical intimacy, attempts he had of course deftly outmanoeuvred—he never mixed business with his private life!—before he was able to find out that the Black Widow, as Cathy called her stepmother, would be in Canada the second week of January, skiing with her daughter, Charlotte.

There was obviously little sisterly love between Cathy and Charlotte either, Cathy referring to her half-sibling as 'the brat'. There had to be an age gap between the two sisters, and at thirty Cathy was already starting to lose her bloom, her blonde beauty, after years of grievance, taking on a certain hardness that was far from attractive, so the existence of a young and probably pretty half-sister wouldn't go down too well with someone like her. Besides which, having grown up in the lap of luxury, with a mother who was patently money-grasping herself, Charlotte Sutherland *was* probably a brat!

'You've done your research on this woman, then, Jarrett?' Alison prompted curiously.

He shrugged. 'I'm only interested in her business life, not her personal one.' Although Cathy would have been only too happy to go on for hours about the woman her father had married after the death of her own mother twenty years ago, if he'd let her! But as far as Jarrett was concerned it was just another example of why marriage wasn't for him. He could imagine nothing worse than being married for his money. By all accounts, Daniel Sutherland had been an intelligent man, and he had still been fooled. For some years, it seemed.

'You still haven't told us what business you have with her?' Abbie said casually.

He shook his head, leaning back in his chair, his expression closed. 'I think I've said altogether too much on the subject already,' he said firmly. 'It must have been the champagne we drank earlier to toast your marriage.' He addressed the other couple.

'Talking of which...'' Stephen signalled the waiter, requesting another bottle of champagne for the four of them.

Which gave Jarrett the few minutes' respite he needed to gather his scattered wits together. He had said enough already, revealed more than necessary of himself and his reasons for being here in Canada. For a man who was usually private to the point of rudeness—even Cathy Sutherland, so free with the information about the stepmother she detested, hadn't known why he was so interested in her!—he felt uncomfortable with the knowledge that he had been provoked into revealing that much to the three people present.

It was Abbie's fault, of course. While giving every appearance of being open and beautiful, she had nevertheless managed not to reveal a single fact about herself, but had goaded Jarrett, he now realised, into talking about himself in an effort to get her to open up about herself.

He tried to think what he did know about her. She had once been a model—years ago, if they coincided with the period he had spent in Australia. She travelled a great deal, and not through choice, if her dislike of it was to be believed. If she didn't like it so much, then why do it at all? She—

He was becoming obsessed with the woman, he realised angrily. And for a man who, at best, viewed women with teasing affection, and at worst with cold disdain, it wasn't a feeling he was particularly comfortable with!

'I think you have an admirer, Abbie.' He dryly changed the subject.

She arched dark brows in cool dismissal. 'But we hardly know each other, Jarrett,' she returned just as dryly.

Golden eyes narrowed on the ivory perfection of her face; was she mocking him? 'I wasn't referring to myself,' he bit back, aware that he sounded rude and disdainful.

She frowned as his meaning became clear to her, looking about them with apprehensive eyes.

And, as she did so, it suddenly hit Jarrett that this woman was running away from something. Or someone...

At the same time as he realised this, Jarrett felt a previously unknown protectiveness. Towards Abbie. A woman, as she had already said, that he hardly knew! But despite her previous cool assurance there was a vulnerability about her at this moment, an air of uncertainty as she worriedly searched the faces of the other diners in the restaurant.

Jarrett sat forward, his face on a level with Abbie's. 'He's seated two tables away, to the left,' he told her quietly. 'And he doesn't seem able to take his eyes off you. Not that I can altogether blame him,' he added. 'It can't be every day that you see Cleopatra and Delilah all wrapped up in one deliciously feminine bundle!'

Abbie had located her admirer now, dismissing the young blond Adonis with one sweep of that violet-blue gaze.

God, she was a cool one, Jarrett acknowledged admiringly. The man who was watching her so intently had

the sort of film-star good looks most women would drool
over, and yet Abbie showed no feminine interest in him
whatsoever, totally controlled again as her attention returned to their table, their main course now being served
to them.

Stephen came into their conversation. 'Cleopatra and
Delilah were both scheming women...'

Jarrett grinned. 'But beautiful, if history is to be believed—very beautiful.'

'If you'll all excuse me for a few minutes.' Abbie
spoke distractedly, seemingly unconcerned at the barb in
Jarrett's remark. 'I have to go and make a telephone
call.' She stood up as she excused herself, picking up
her small clutch-bag, to walk across the restaurant and
out into the lobby beyond, where public telephones were
situated.

'Was it something I said...?' Jarrett asked his two
remaining dinner companions.

'I doubt it,' Stephen replied. 'Abbie probably does just
have to make a telephone call.'

Maybe she did, Jarrett inwardly acknowledged, but
the man who had been seated two tables away, the man
who had been watching her so avidly through the meal,
had obviously seen her departure as an opportunity to
actually speak to her, getting up himself and following
her from the room!

Jarrett's eyes became golden slits as he watched the
other man, whose hurried departure, so soon after
Abbie's, his meal half-eaten, couldn't just be a coincidence. Despite Abbie's air of cool assurance, there was
also that vulnerability Jarrett had recognised in her earlier, and the delicacy of her tall, willowy body. The man
who had followed her, so opportunely, was very tall and

muscular, looked as if he worked out just for the hell of it!

He put his own snowy white linen napkin down on the table beside Abbie's. 'I'll be back in a moment,' he muttered, eyes narrowed purposefully as he strode out of the restaurant, uncaring of what Stephen and Alison thought of his departure.

It didn't take him long to locate Abbie. Or the blond Adonis.

They were standing together across the lobby, nowhere near the public telephone booths, which were on the other side of the wide marbled hall. And even as Jarrett went to march across it and put a stop to the blond man's intrusion Abbie reached up and put her hand on her companion's arm in a gesture of familiarity, her smile warm and relaxed as she looked up into that handsome face.

Jarrett came to an abrupt halt, a knot tightening in his stomach while he watched the continuing conversation between the couple. Although she had given no indication of it earlier when he'd pointed the other man out to her, Abbie knew that blond giant! There was a familiarity between them that spoke of an intimacy of long standing; Abbie was looking quite animated now.

Jarrett felt a wave of temper sweep through him at the way Abbie was behaving with the other man. The two had behaved like strangers in the restaurant, no sign of familiarity between them, despite the fact that the man hadn't seemed able to take his eyes off Abbie. What the hell was going on?

Whatever it was, Jarrett didn't intend being caught standing here staring at the two of them like a gawking schoolboy!

Yet as their conversation continued he found he

couldn't move away. The two of them were very animated now, the man talking softly, but obviously slightly aggressively, while Abbie slowly shook her head in disagreement with what he was saying. The man broke off abruptly, and Abbie spoke to him now, that hand reassuringly on his arm once again. The man seemed to sigh his capitulation at what was being said, murmuring some sort of agreement, and Abbie nodded, a smile hovering about her sensuous lips.

The woman wasn't just a mystery, she was an enigma, and Jarrett had too much else on his mind at the moment to try to get to the bottom of it. Maybe Abbie, for all she was such an old friend of Alison's, was actually a high-class call-girl; it would certainly fit in with her reluctance to talk about herself, and the fact that she travelled so much without really enjoying it. It would also explain the single name of Abbie...

It did fit too, only too well, he slowly realised. A woman of Abbie's undoubted beauty would be well sought after, could probably name her own price for the possession of that cool, elusive beauty, no matter how fleetingly.

Hell, he had probably spent the best part of the evening lusting after a woman who sold what he wanted from her! But he had never paid for a woman in his life—at least, not with cold, hard cash. Although expensive jewellery at the end of a brief relationship probably amounted to the same thing.

Oh, to hell with this, he inwardly cursed; if that was what she was he might as well have her himself for the night, and once he had he could get on with concentrating on the real reason he was here.

That decision made, he turned on his heel and walked back into the restaurant. Whatever arrangements Abbie was making to meet the blond Adonis later, she could damn well break. The only man she was going home with tonight was him. And it would be a night he intended them both to remember!

He watched her intently as she negotiated around the tables to where her party was seated, half expecting his desire for her to have lessened with the knowledge of what he now thought she was. But it hadn't, the gently swaying hips, firm up-thrusting breasts, pert beneath the fitted sheath of her dress, only succeeded in evoking vivid images in his mind. Damn it, he had never wanted a woman as much as he now wanted Abbie—no matter what she was!

'You shouldn't have waited for me,' she commented as she sat down, looking pointedly at Jarrett's untouched steak.

His mouth twisted. 'I didn't. I've only just returned to the table myself,' he added after a deliberate pause, observing her under hooded lids. And he wasn't disappointed. She gave him a startled look, instantly wary, he realised with satisfaction.

'Oh?'

She had to be wondering where he had been, to have just returned himself, must also be wondering if he had seen her talking to the blond Adonis. Well she could sit and wonder!

'Successful telephone call?' he said lightly before cutting into his perfectly cooked steak, seemingly uninterested in her answer. Because he knew she hadn't made any telephone call!

'Er—yes,' she confirmed abruptly, still looking at him uncertainly.

'Everything okay?' Alison put in gently.

Abbie's expression softened as she turned to her friend. 'Everything is fine,' she nodded warmly.

Were Alison and Stephen aware of what this woman did? Somehow he doubted it. Oh, Stephen was no angel, had been involved with lots of women before meeting Alison a few years ago, and Alison herself admitted to several relationships before Stephen. But what Abbie did was something else entirely, and certainly couldn't be classed as relationships!

It was with a certain amount of satisfaction that Jarrett noticed the continued absence of the blond Adonis from his chair two tables away. The man, his business, he believed, successfully concluded, hadn't even bothered to return and finish his meal. Well, he was going to regret later having missed out on his meal, and on Abbie—because Jarrett had plans of his own where she was concerned. And it was very rare for him not to get what he wanted!

The rest of the evening dragged as far as Jarrett was concerned, the exquisitely prepared food tasteless to him, his lack of contribution to the conversation drawing several veiled glances from those violet-blue eyes beneath long black lashes. Much to his satisfaction. He might as well be as much of a mystery to her as she was to him!

All the time his tension was rising, his anticipation of the night ahead making him completely introspective.

He had no idea how one went about paying a woman to go to bed with one.

But the blond Adonis had seemed to have no trouble arranging it, so neither would he!

CHAPTER THREE

ABBIE was all too aware of the brooding silence of the man sitting next to her, and of his steadily increasing tension.

But she had no logical explanation for his behaviour.

Oh, she had been a little concerned when he'd mentioned leaving the table at the same time she had, had wondered if he could have seen her out in the lobby talking to Tony. But, she had decided, even if he had witnessed that conversation, it would merely have looked as if the man who couldn't 'take his eyes off her' had tried to strike up an acquaintance with her when he'd seen the opportunity of finding her on her own. And, as Tony hadn't returned to his table, it would seem that he must have been rebuffed.

No, it couldn't have been that which had changed Jarrett's mood. Because it *had* changed. Unless his long silences were his way of sticking to his promise about keeping his cynicism to himself? She had wondered how he was going to manage that, when he obviously viewed life through such jaundiced eyes. Perhaps he had decided silence was the best course of action!

Not that she in the least minded his lack of participation in the conversation. She had been totally stunned earlier when he'd revealed that she—well, actually Sabina Sutherland—was the reason for his coming to Whistler. Although Alison had assured her, once they'd reached the powder-room, after Abbie's choking fit, that neither she nor Stephen had been aware of Jarrett's rea-

son for being here, either. Nor did they know what b..
ness Jarrett had with Sabina Sutherland.

Jarrett was an entrepreneur—for that Abbie read opportunist!—with a finger in many pies. But as
Sutherlands were also a multi-business company that
told Abbie absolutely nothing. However, by the time
Abbie returned to her private ski-lodge somewhere up
the mountain, she should have all the information on
Jarrett Hunter that she would need, in order to know
whether or not she should see him as Sabina
Sutherland...

She sincerely hoped the answer to that proved to be
negative. Jarrett Hunter wasn't a man she felt in the least
comfortable with, and dealing with him on a business
level would be like handling the unleashed tiger his eyes
so reminded her of!

Eyes that watched her whenever he thought she was
concentrating her interest elsewhere. And his interest
was purely male, seeming to concentrate on each of her
physical attributes in turn. She was sure she had been
mentally stripped naked, and then reclothed, in the last
hour!

'Can I see you safely back to your suite?' he offered
smoothly later as they all left the restaurant together.
'I'm sure Alison and Stephen are more than ready to
disappear after this interruption to their honeymoon.'

Abbie delayed answering him as she smiled her
thanks at the young man who had just returned her jacket
and overcoat to her, the latter an expensive copy of a
sable—she couldn't stand the thought of wearing a real
fur that had once covered some poor luckless animal's
body, but the icy Canadian winter called for warmth as
well as comfort.

She wrapped the ankle-length coat about her before

releasing her hair from the confines of its collar, turning to smile coolly at Jarrett. 'As you can see by this coat,' she commented, turning up the collar to keep her neck warm, 'I'm not a guest at this hotel.'

He looked deeply irritated by this turn of events, scowling darkly. 'Then perhaps I can see you back to the hotel you are staying at?' he grated.

'There's no need,' she dismissed, turning to hug first Alison and then Stephen. 'It's been lovely seeing you both. And dinner was lovely, too. I'll return the compliment when we're all back in London,' she added, before at last turning back to Jarrett Hunter, holding out her hand in formal parting. 'It was nice to meet you, Mr Hunter.' Politeness demanded that she say at least that much!

His mouth twisted, the golden eyes full of scepticism as he took hold of the hand she held out so graciously. 'Was it?' he returned with dry derision, obviously not fooled by her politeness for a minute.

She gave a short nod of confirmation. 'It's always interesting to meet someone else from home on one's travels, Mr Hunter,' she returned noncommittally, pointedly removing her hand from his when he made no effort to release her.

He looked at her sharply. 'If you miss home so much, perhaps you shouldn't do so much—travelling.'

She met his gaze unflinchingly, not in the least sure what he meant by that remark—except that it had somehow sounded like a put-down! 'I go where I'm needed,' she clipped. 'Now I really do have to go.'

'I said I would like to see you home,' Jarrett repeated with soft intent. 'It's late, and you shouldn't go alone—'

'But I'm not going alone, Mr Hunter; I have a car waiting for me outside,' she said, the edge of the resistance she was feeling at his persistence creeping into her voice. For goodness' sake, couldn't he understand? She didn't want his company, back to her hotel, or anywhere else for that matter!

His mouth tightened, a nerve pulsing in his jaw, his eyes suddenly pure molten gold. 'In that case, I'll walk you to your car.' And without waiting for her agreement, or otherwise, he took a firm grasp of her arm, almost frogmarching her through the lobby.

Abbie turned briefly to give Alison and Stephen a last wave goodbye, Alison giving her a puzzled stare, Stephen frowning.

Which wasn't surprising, when Jarrett was almost dragging her out of the hotel!

Abbie came to an abrupt halt on the pavement outside, her car already parked there waiting for her departure. 'You're behaving very—strangely, Mr Hunter,' she snapped, releasing herself from his vice-like grip as she turned to face him.

'*I'm* behaving strangely!' he returned incredulously, eyes gleaming golden in the lamplight that shone from the front of the hotel.

Whistler was a small community that had grown into existence mainly because of the wonderful skiing conditions on Whistler Mountain, and its near neighbour, Blackcomb. The village itself had been designed more like a Swiss village, with double-storey chalet-type buildings. The hotels that thrived in the area had also been built to reflect this uniqueness, and at the moment Christmas lights still adorned trees and buildings. It was almost like a fairy-tale—and yet Abbie was starting to feel as if she was in the middle of a horror story!

'I believe so,' she answered slowly, watching Jarrett warily, but also aware that Tim, her dark-haired driver, was only feet away, seated behind the wheel of the car, if she should need his assistance. Which she sincerely hoped she wouldn't. Being at the centre of a brawl, outside one of her own hotels, would not help in keeping the low-key existence she preferred to lead. 'I have to go—'

'You already said that,' Jarrett rasped. 'Several times, in fact.' He looked past her to the parked, chauffeur-driven limousine, his expression instantly scornful. 'He obviously has money,' he drawled contemptuously.

Abbie frowned her bewilderment at the comment, starting to wonder if perhaps champagne didn't agree with this man; he had seemed relatively comprehensible—too much so with regard to his opinion of women!—before he had drunk it. 'Who does?' she prompted dazedly.

'The blond Adonis,' Jarrett continued harshly. 'Whatever he's worth, Abbie, I'm sure I'm worth more!'

'I'm sure you are,' she agreed soothingly, her bewilderment deepening. What blond Adonis? 'It's late, Jarrett—'

'But it's going to get a lot later for you, isn't it?' he bit out accusingly, glaring down at her. 'Why do you do it, Abbie? Don't tell me you actually enjoy it!' he added disgustedly.

Champagne obviously didn't agree with him; he wasn't making any sense at all now. She gave a barely perceptible movement to indicate Tim should come and open the car door for her now. 'I'm sure one of us is going to be suffering with a terrible headache in the morning,' she told Jarrett lightly. 'And it isn't going to be me!' she amended before climbing thankfully into the back of the white limousine.

Jarrett stepped forward and stopped Tim closing the

door behind her. 'Are you implying I'm drunk, Abbie?' he growled.

'I'm implying that one of us needs to sober up—and again it isn't me!' She nodded to Tim to close the car door, sitting back with some relief when, with one last scathing glare, Jarrett stepped back before turning on his heel and striding back into the hotel. In the direction of the bar, no doubt!

Abbie gave a weary sigh, relaxing back against the limousine's leather upholstery. It had been a very long evening. And it wasn't over yet...

Lights blazed in the chalet ski-lodge she had rented for her stay at Whistler, but thankfully not at the back, where Charlie's bedroom was; her young daughter should have been asleep hours ago.

She nodded her thanks distractedly to Tim as she got out of the car, running lightly up the steps to let herself inside the lodge, going straight through to the lounge where she knew Tony would be waiting for her.

He looked up as she came in. He was sitting at a table working on some papers he had laid out there, the flames from the log fire giving his hair the colour of rich cream. 'Everything okay?' he prompted worriedly as Abbie stood in the doorway staring at him.

'Fine,' she replied. 'Charlie?'

He gave an affectionate smile as he stood up. 'Asleep. But looking forward to skiing in the morning,' he added warningly.

Abbie smiled too now. Her daughter had been able to ski almost as soon as she could walk, and it took all of Abbie's efforts to keep up with her. But Charlie never seemed to tire of skiing, making run after run.

However, it was something else that held Abbie's attention now. Tony was blond and athletically built...

Could he be the blond Adonis Jarrett Hunter had been so scathing about? Jarrett had left the table this evening soon after she had departed to make her 'phone call', returning only seconds before her; could he have seen her out in the lobby talking to Tony? And if so, what conclusions had he come to after seeing the two of them together?

She tried to think back to the strange conversation she'd had with Jarrett outside the hotel, something about 'he obviously has money', and that he—Jarrett—was 'worth more', and the night was going to be 'a lot later' for her, and she didn't actually enjoy it—

Good God, Jarrett Hunter thought she was a—! Abbie began to laugh. He did! Jarrett thought she had been making an assignation with Tony, an assignation for which she was going to be paid!

Tony gave her a quizzical look as she continued to laugh, totally confused as to the reason for it. And, in the circumstances, Abbie wasn't about to explain them, either!

Tony worked for her; he was part minder—which was why he had been in the restaurant at all this evening— and part personal assistant. He had worked for her for two years now, and never, ever had he even tried to step over their employee-employer relationship and into intimacy.

Abbie had never wanted him to, either. Oh, Tony was certainly good-looking enough, and at thirty he was close to her own age of twenty-seven, but, as she had stated only too clearly earlier, she didn't have a sweet tooth!

Her husband had died two years ago, and since that time there had been no man in her life, not even on such a casual basis as the odd dinner. And that was the way she liked it, the way it was going to remain.

Although Jarrett Hunter obviously had her marked down as something else completely…!

She sobered slowly, shaking her head as Tony still looked at her questioningly. 'It was just something that happened earlier,' she said as she took off her coat and threw it over the back of a chair. 'Did you get that information I asked for?' she asked briskly.

'It's here.' He picked up the file from the top of the table which he had been working on. 'It isn't complete yet, but the rest should come through some time tomorrow. But what we already have makes interesting reading,' he informed her pointedly.

She nodded, taking the file when he held it out to her. 'I'll take it to bed with me.'

Tony grinned. 'I've always admired the way you can be up half the night working, and then still emerge the next morning looking fresh as a daisy!'

Abbie grimaced. 'Remind me of that tomorrow night after I've been skiing with Charlie all day!'

She left Tony chuckling to himself as she went down the hallway to check on Charlie before going to her own bedroom.

Charlie was fast asleep in her bed, a miniature version of Abbie, her long dark hair fanned out across the pillow, her tiny face angelic in the moonlight, one of her arms wrapped about the teddy-bear she always took to bed with her—Abbie forgot to pack that teddy at her peril! It had been mislaid when they'd been unpacking after a business trip a few months ago, and Charlie had been inconsolable until it was found again.

Abbie bent down and kissed her daughter on the forehead, lovingly smoothing back the feathered fringe of dark hair. Charlie meant everything to her, and the time was fast approaching when her young daughter would have to start school. The two of them were inseparable, and it was going to be a wrench for both of them when Charlie was at school for five days of the week.

Abbie gave a resigned sigh, giving one last wistful look at her daughter before leaving the room. For Charlie's sake she had to be positive about the prospect of going to school, but for her own she never wanted September to arrive!

Ten minutes later, her make-up removed, her hair slightly damp from her shower, Abbie sat up in bed with the file Tony had given her earlier. And Jarrett Hunter, the subject of the file, believed she was awake in bed somewhere doing something much more strenuous than reading! And getting paid for it. What an amazing cynic he was, to have come to such a conclusion about her, on so little evidence.

Ten minutes later, when she had finished reading what information Tony had been able to get on Jarrett at such short notice, Abbie still thought the word 'amazing' applied to him. Jarrett Hunter was an oldest son; his parents' marriage had been stormy by the look of it, and when his father had gone bankrupt at forty his wife had walked out on him and their three sons, leaving her husband to pick up the pieces of his shattered business as well as his private life, and to bring up the boys as best he could.

Luckily Jarrett had just completed his A levels at a private school, but his two younger brothers, aged sixteen and fourteen, had had to be placed in state school to finish their education. Jarrett had chosen not to take up the place he had easily obtained at a university, but instead had gone out to work so that he could contribute to the family coffers. It was here his history became a bit hazy, until he'd emerged onto the business scene about eight years later as the owner of hotels and leisure complexes all over England, at which time he had shifted his interest to Australia, opening up similar businesses there.

Tony was right—the file wasn't complete; the five years since Jarrett Hunter's return to England weren't yet accounted for. And they were the key to why he wanted to see Sabina Sutherland, Abbie was sure. Although his interest in hotels gave her some idea of what his mission might be...

She closed the file, resting her head back against the pillow. What an amazing history the man had. He had built up a multi-million-pound empire from virtually nothing, both his brothers now working with him, his father having retired and now living in Australia with his second wife—this marriage, it seemed, much happier than the first.

Abbie now had the answer as to why Jarrett Hunter had such contempt for women, and a complete aversion to marriage. With a mother like his, it wasn't surprising he didn't trust or like women very much!

But still Abbie was curious about those five years since Jarrett moved back to England...

'Isn't this just lovely, Mummy?' Charlie, tall for only four years of age, looked up and grinned at her mother, the two of them making their way over to the ski-lift at Blackcomb for their first run of the day.

At only just nine o'clock in the morning, the lifts were still quite empty, the majority of skiers usually arriving mid-morning. Which was why Abbie preferred to come up here early, hoping to avoid the crowds of the day, if she could. And she knew that Tony was sitting in the coffee-shop not far away at the bottom of the mountain, ever vigilant, in spite of his supposedly relaxed pose as he warmed his hands about his cup of coffee. Nevertheless, Abbie still didn't like being in places so full of people. But Charlie loved to ski, as evidenced by the radiant pleasure on her face as the two of them waited their turn to go up on the ski-lift. And, as much as was possible, Abbie wanted Charlie to grow up enjoying the freedom life had to offer her.

'Lovely, darling,' Abbie echoed lightly, as Tony had predicted, none the worse for her late night.

Mother and daughter were dressed in identical white fitted ski-suits and ski-boots, the darkness of their hair hidden beneath white fur hats that framed the delicacy of their features, the clearness of their skin, and the glow in both sets of violet-blue eyes almost giving them the appearance of sisters rather than mother and daughter.

It was almost time for them to sit on the chair-lift now, and they moved their poles and set their skis straight ready to move forward into position, Charlie having been persuaded to attempt one of the lower slopes before venturing further up the mountain.

'Mind if I join you, ladies?' a cheerful voice enquired even as the black-suited figure skied into place beside Charlie.

Abbie hadn't been aware of him anywhere near, but as she looked at the confident grin on Jarrett Hunter's face she knew that he had deliberately timed his moment so that all they could do was move forward as a trio and let the ski-lift scoop them up.

She glanced back at the coffee-shop where Tony sat, just in time to see him come rushing out of the door, a worried frown darkening his handsome face. Abbie gave a barely perceptible shake of her head, acknowledged thankfully by Tony's raised hand, before she turned back to Jarrett Hunter.

What was he doing here? When they had parted last night he hadn't given the impression he particularly wanted to see her again; instead it had seemed that, believing he had assessed her true profession, and been rebuffed by her, she could go to hell for all he cared—if she wasn't there already!

Unless he had discovered, in the last ten hours, exactly what her real identity was; that might be a good enough reason for his behaviour this morning!

He held out his hand in a friendly gesture to Charlie. 'Hi, I'm Jarrett.'

Her daughter grinned at him unabashedly, holding out her own tiny gloved hand. 'I'm Charlie,' she supplied shyly. 'And this is my mummy.'

That golden gaze mockingly met Abbie's over the top of the child's head. 'Hello, Mummy,' he drawled dryly.

She nodded coolly, extremely wary, but not wanting to alarm Charlie. 'Jarrett.'

The rest of the information she had requested on this man still hadn't arrived, but she already knew enough about him to realise he usually got where he wanted, and when he wanted—and at the moment he wanted to be on this chair-lift with Charlie and herself!

Charlie giggled. 'Her name isn't really Mummy,' she chided with a smile. 'Only I call her Mummy.'

Jarrett raised dark brows, having shunned wearing a ski-hat, his goggles pushed back into the darkness of his hair. 'Does that mean you don't have any brothers or sisters?' he teased.

Abbie held her breath as she waited for Charlie's answer. God knew Cathy and Danny, Daniel's children from his first marriage, were obnoxious enough whenever they saw Charlie, but that didn't mean her daughter didn't consider them her sister and brother...!

Charlie shook her head, very serious for a four-year-old. 'I'm Mummy's special little girl.' She repeated parrot-fashion what Abbie had been telling her since the day she was born.

Because Charlie was special: bright, as well as beautiful, with a loving nature and lack of guile that boded well for the time she was old enough to pick up the reins of her own inheritance. But until that time Abbie intended protecting her as best she could...

'I can quite understand why,' Jarrett answered Charlie. 'You're gorgeous—like your mummy!'

Abbie frowned across at him as Charlie gave a delighted laugh; did he know yet that she was Sabina Sutherland? His completely innocent gaze as he met hers said he was up to something—but it didn't reveal what it was. Well, if he thought he could get to her by being charming to her daughter, he was going to be out of luck. Until she knew more about him, she had no intention of talking to him as Sabina Sutherland!

'Here we go,' Jarrett warned as they approached the end of the chair-lift. 'Can she manage?' he questioned Abbie softly as Charlie straightened in her seat, poles ready in her hands.

Abbie gave a rueful grimace. 'Better than us probably!'

Which Charlie promptly demonstrated as she glided easily away from the chair-lift, already poised for her run down the mountain.

'I see what you mean!' Jarrett nodded as the two of them made a less elegant exit from the chair-lift, looking on with admiration as the little girl stood a little way off. 'Kids know no fear, do they?' He gave a rueful shake of his head.

A shadow passed over Abbie's face as she too looked across at her young daughter. 'At only four years old, she shouldn't even be aware what fear is, Mr Hunter,' she snapped.

'It was Jarrett last night,' he murmured huskily. 'During the latter part of the evening, anyway...!'

Abbie drew in a sharp breath, quickly dispelling any dark thoughts she might have just had. 'How's your head this morning?' she derided.

He raised mocking brows. 'Clear as a bell. How's yours?'

'The same,' she responded. 'I slept very well,' she added, her expression challenging.

A scowl instantly darkened his features. 'You—'

'Mummy, can we go down now?' Charlie cut in eagerly, her body still poised impatiently.

Abbie's mouth twisted wryly as she gave Jarrett an apologetic smile. 'Children have no patience, either!' she told him as she adjusted her poles in her hands and moved her sunglasses down over her eyes to cut out some of the glare of the newly fallen snow, ready for her own run.

Jarrett was still looking across at Charlie. 'I had no idea you had a child...' he said slowly.

No doubt he must imagine that could make things a little difficult for her at times—in her profession! 'There are a lot of things you don't know about me, Jarrett,' she returned dryly. 'Just as some of the things you think you know aren't true, either.'

Those golden eyes narrowed. 'Such as?'

She ignored his question. 'Charlie is waiting,' she prompted.

'I'll see you at the bottom,' he called out as he skied off and left them both, his sure movements telling of years of skiing experience.

'He's good, Mummy,' Charlie said admiringly as she watched him.

Abbie very much doubted the word 'good' was very often applied to Jarrett Hunter—except possibly by the legion of women that seemed to have been briefly in his life over the years. But Abbie certainly wasn't interested in his sexual prowess, good or otherwise!

However, his skiing was excellent, Abbie conceded as she followed him and Charlie at a more sedate pace— she had the rest of the day to get through yet, no point in tiring herself from the onset, just to prove to Jarrett Hunter that she was as good a skier as he was.

She could see the ever watchful figure of Tony standing at the bottom of the slope as he monitored their progress, the bright blue of his jacket easily discernible.

Charlie, with her much lighter build, had easily caught up with Jarrett, the two of them now skiing together, Charlie then completely confident as she easily took the lead. Abbie had a feeling that Jarrett might have let her do that; from the way he had skied away from them a few minutes ago he had reached a professional level.

She arrived at the base of the mountain seconds behind, snow spraying up as she came to a halt only feet away from the two of them, emotion catching in her throat at the way Charlie grinned up so openly at Jarrett. Whatever the cost to herself the last two years, it had all been worth it to see that completely trusting look on her daughter's face.

Tony walked over to them quickly, his gaze narrowed on Jarrett as the other man pushed his goggles up into the thickness of his hair. Tony was obviously not at all pleased with the way Jarrett had insinuated himself onto the ski-lift with them.

'Everything okay, Mrs Sutherland?' Tony enquired tightly, obviously having recognised Jarrett now from the evening before.

Abbie didn't need to see the sudden tension in Jarrett Hunter's body—she could feel it! He hadn't known her real identity until this moment!

And from the expression in his eyes as he looked at her, and from the tightening of his mouth, he was far from pleased at knowing it now!

Considering the things he had said about Sabina Sutherland the evening before, that wasn't surprising!

CHAPTER FOUR

JARRETT stared at the woman he had just been informed was Sabina Sutherland

Sabina—Abbie…

Charlie—Charlotte…

Hell!

How on earth could he possibly have known that Abbie was a diminutive of Sabina?

But Stephen and Alison had certainly known—and instead of putting him straight had let him continue to make a fool of himself! The woman he had told them he had been chasing after for months had actually been sitting right next to him at the time!

How the hell could he have known, have even begun to guess? Cathy spoke of her stepmother in such aggressive terms—but she had never once mentioned that Sabina was younger than she was! Or that 'the brat' Charlotte was only four years old. And, from the little Jarrett had seen of Charlie this morning, she didn't seem to be a brat at all…

He looked at Abbie—Sabina—once again. She was beautiful, there was no doubting that, and she was only Alison's age, in her late twenties at the most, and yet he knew Daniel Sutherland had been fifty-eight when he died two years ago—more than thirty years older than his wife. What was the saying, 'there's no fool like an old fool'? Daniel Sutherland must have been insane—or just totally besotted—to have married a woman more than thirty years his junior!

Which posed the question, why had Abbie married him? That question was so simple to answer it wasn't even worth asking; Daniel Sutherland's fortune had been estimated to be at the fifty-million-pound mark when he died! Abbie, the employee's daughter, had become Sabina Sutherland, a very rich and powerful lady. And he used that last word advisedly; Abbie might not exactly be what he had thought her last night, but she was certainly no lady, either!

He drew in a harshly controlling breath. 'Very amusing,' he rasped contemptuously. 'You must all have had a good laugh last night—at my expense!'

Violet-blue eyes met his cooly. 'I can assure you that no one was laughing last night—either with you or at you.'

'Why the subterfuge in the first place?' he growled. 'Or is that the way you enjoy mixing with the peasants occasionally?' he added scathingly.

The blond Adonis stepped forward threateningly at Jarrett's aggressive tone, but Abbie stayed him with a gentle raising of her hand. 'It's okay, Tony, I can handle this,' she assured him. 'Perhaps you would like to take Charlie on her next run?'

It was made as a suggestion, but nevertheless it was obvious that Tony accepted it for the order it undoubtedly was, taking Charlie along with him as he went to collect his skis, all the time keeping a watchful eye on Jarrett.

The man wasn't Abbie's lover, damn it, he was her minder!

That was the reason he had been watching her so avidly in the restaurant the evening before, why Abbie had met him out in the lobby and dismissed him for the evening when Jarrett had picked up on his interest. Why he was here watching Abbie and Charlie this morning.

Jarrett had seen Tony arrive on the ski slope with Abbie and the little girl, watched as Tony went off to the coffee-shop, biding his own time so that he could join the two females at a point when Tony couldn't intervene.

The question was, why did Abbie need a minder in the first place?

As far as Jarrett had been able to make out from Cathy's resentful mutterings, Daniel Sutherland hadn't been a complete fool where his second wife was concerned and had left his considerable fortune to be shared between his three children; forty-nine per cent of his business interests had been divided equally between Cathy and Danny, the lion's share of fifty-one per cent going to his youngest child, Charlotte, to be administered by her mother, Sabina, until she was twenty-one, at which time Charlotte would take over her own inheritance.

But Jarrett hadn't realised Charlotte was so young when her father died, only two years old, and a lot could happen to her fortune and shares in nineteen years...

But in the meantime Sabina Sutherland was the one who wielded the power. Perhaps she did need a minder, after all...!

'There was no subterfuge, Mr Hunter.' Sabina Sutherland now answered his question. 'I am an old friend of Alison's, since our modelling days together. And most people call me Abbie,' she added.

Cathy certainly didn't. The Black Widow was how she referred to her stepmother. And Danny, at only twenty-six, weak and a wastrel, referred to her as 'dear Stepmama'. And, in view of the fact that Jarrett now knew the two were of a similar age, it was far from a respectful way of addressing her. Was it any wonder, with these descriptions of the woman, that Jarrett had been expecting Sabina Sutherland to be a combination of Lucretia Borgia and Mata Hari?

Instead he was faced with the most beautiful woman he had ever seen in his life, a woman he still wanted, despite knowing exactly who she was...!

'I believe there is something you wish to discuss with me?' She spoke softly now, as if half guessing what was on his mind.

Only half guessing, because if she had known all the thoughts that were going through his head she wouldn't look quite so calm!

He wanted this woman. He had known that only too forcibly this morning when he'd woken up at six o'clock, after a fitful night's sleep, his dreams full of a naked Abbie in the arms of the blond Adonis, and realised he still desired her, even if he thought she had just spent the night with another man. Although after the way they had parted the evening before he didn't think she particularly wanted to see him again!

He hadn't been able to believe his luck when he'd spotted her standing near the coffee-shop earlier, although he had been a little surprised at the presence of a little girl, and incensed at the blond Adonis being there too. Although he had taken his chance to approach her when the other man went off to have coffee...

He still couldn't believe it! Sabina Sutherland. She was more beautiful than any woman had a right to be. Perhaps Daniel Sutherland hadn't been insane, after all. Or, if he had, Jarrett had a feeling he was heading the same way!

'Jarrett…?' she prompted as he made no response to her earlier comment.

He blinked, clearing his head of the desire that was threatening to blind him to who and what this woman was. 'I do,' he confirmed harshly. 'But it's a business meeting.' His mouth twisted. 'And it can hardly be discussed here.' He looked about them; the slopes and ski-lifts were rapidly filling up now with chattering, happy skiers.

'Perhaps I could meet you at the hotel later today?' But she looked doubtful even as she said it.

'I'm supposed to be meeting Alison and Stephen this afternoon—although it should be a very short meeting! Just long enough for me to punch him on the nose for not telling me last night who you are!' His eyes glittered angrily just at the thought of the conversations he had so innocently been a part of the previous evening. 'Some friend he is!'

Abbie gave a smile. 'It seems a pity to do anything so drastic on his honeymoon. Besides,' she added, 'they were only protecting my privacy.'

He accepted that, realised she was a very private person, but even so Stephen could have warned him of the tangle he was getting himself into, had had plenty of opportunity to do exactly that when the two ladies had disappeared to the powder-room. Immediately after Abbie had almost choked because he had told them it was Sabina Sutherland whom he was here to meet…

He hated feeling at a disadvantage like this! And those interminable dinners with Cathy Sutherland had been a complete waste of time too, in view of the way he had finally met his quarry. Hell, he remembered that somewhere in the conversation last night he had implied this woman had all the substance of a chocolate éclair!

Where had that conversation come from? There was something about Abbie that openly challenged him, he inwardly admitted. He couldn't remember reacting this strongly to a woman for a long time—if ever!

'Well, they succeeded,' he rasped harshly. 'But now I've been left with egg on my face!'

Abbie seemed surprised. 'It doesn't show.'

'Well, believe me, I can feel it,' he bit out hardly. 'But despite all that I do have some business I would like to talk to you about. Perhaps we could have dinner together this evening? Just the two of us this time,' he added. 'With everyone knowing exactly who they are!'

'I've always known who I am, Jarrett,' Abbie assured him quietly. 'But I left Charlie last night, so I really would prefer not to leave her again tonight.'

'I want to talk to you, Abbie,' Jarrett said determinedly.

She looked irritated by his persistence. 'In that case, you will have to come to my ski-lodge, and we can talk there. I'll send my car for you.'

So that she didn't have to tell him her exact location. And if they were on her home ground her minder would be in close attendance; Jarrett very much doubted Abbie intended being alone with him!

'We can talk over dinner,' he pronounced.

She looked far from pleased at his sheer bloody-mindedness, violet-blue eyes cloudy, a frown marring the perfection of her brow. 'Is that really necessary?' she finally answered.

This woman did absolutely nothing for his ego, Jarrett ruefully acknowledged. Although, at the same time, her lack of enthusiasm was a refreshing change after some of the women he had known over the years. If only he didn't find Abbie Sutherland so damned desirable!

'We both have to eat, Abbie,' he shrugged.

She still frowned. 'But not together.'

He grinned, he just couldn't help himself; she was infuriating. Beautiful—but infuriating. 'Have you been involved in many relationships since your husband's death, Abbie?' he enquired, still not a hundred per cent sure of the role of the blond Adonis in her life.

The startled look of revulsion on her face was enough to make him sure, very sure. But now he was curious about that revulsion. On top of her claim that she didn't have a sweet tooth it was very curious indeed.

Was it possible she had actually loved her husband, and that was the reason there had been no relationships since his death? It would be just his luck to find a woman he wanted as badly as he wanted this one, only to find she was still in love with her dead husband!

No, he didn't believe that was the case here. The man had been thirty years her senior, and the photographs Jarrett had seen of him did not show him as looking young for his years.

But none of that altered the fact that there had been no man in Abbie's life since his death...

'You said a business discussion, Mr Hunter,' she clipped, every muscle in her body seeming taut. 'I suggest we keep to that. My car will call for you at the hotel at seven-thirty.' And with that she turned and skied away to where Charlie and the blond Adonis had just completed their run down the mountain.

Jarrett watched her go, his eyes narrowed thoughtfully as he did so. Cool and distant, but he had touched a nerve somewhere just now with his question about men in her life, so the lovely Sabina Sutherland wasn't as untouchable as she would like to think she was...

Although verbally wasn't the way Jarrett wanted to touch her!

The white limousine arrived promptly at the hotel at seven-thirty, the driver getting out and coming round the car to open the back door for Jarrett to get in, the man's expression deadpan, but there was, nevertheless, a tell-tale tightness about his unsmiling mouth, a tension in the broadness of his shoulders. For all that she was the elusive Sabina Sutherland, Abbie engendered a loyalty in her employees that threatened physical violence to anyone who looked as if they might harm her.

Jarrett didn't want to harm her, he had something much more pleasurable in mind!

Jarrett grinned at the man unabashedly as he got into the back of the limousine. 'Thanks,' he had time to murmur before the man closed the door firmly behind him—not quite a slam, but it was certainly more forceful than was necessary.

And the glass divider between the back and the front of the car was firmly closed. Not that Jarrett particularly minded that either, being lost in his own thoughts, and not inclined towards conversation.

He had met Stephen and Alison this afternoon as arranged, the couple due to go back to England the following day, their honeymoon over. Stephen had been unrepentant about his part in last night's subterfuge, shrugging it off, with the comment that if Abbie had wanted him to know who she was then she would have told him herself. Alison had been a little more forthcoming than that, defending her friend, and warning Jarrett against causing her any more grief. It was the 'any more' that intrigued him...

What 'grief'—apart from her husband dying two years

ago—could a woman of Sabina Sutherland's beauty and wealth possibly have encountered in her twenty-seven years? That was just one of the many things Jarrett wanted to know about her...

Lights blazed from inside the ski-lodge as Jarrett stepped out of the car, the steps up to the door clear of snow, even though it had been falling lightly for most of the day.

Tony opened the door to him, his expression even more deadpan than the chauffeur's had been, although his tone was polite enough as he took Jarrett through to the sitting-room. But again there was that leashed tension about the other man, warning Jarrett that if he stepped out of line, by even an inch, he would have Tony to answer to.

Jarrett had been expecting this, could easily dismiss it—what he hadn't been expecting was, as he entered the sitting-room, to find Abbie rolling about on the carpet with Charlie as mother and daughter tried to tickle each other!

He felt that fast becoming familiar physical reaction to the natural beauty and allure of this totally fascinating woman, wondering what it was about Abbie that caused him to react so instinctively. This was the third time in two days he had felt uncomfortable with his own arousal, having reacted exactly the same way this morning on the ski-slope. So much for the claimed effect of a cold shower—the freezing temperature this morning had done nothing to alleviate his response!

Abbie sat up, as if she sensed she and Charlie were no longer alone, some of her hair having escaped from the long plait she wore down her spine, so that it fell in wispy tendrils about her make-upless face, the beauty of that face somehow more enhanced by its lack of cosmetics, rather than detracted from.

She was dressed in a loose-fitting white shirt and hugging black leggings, and Jarrett was damn sure she wore nothing beneath the former, her breasts pert and enticing beneath the thin cotton material.

Jarrett realised he wanted nothing more than to make love to her here and now, on the carpet in front of the glowing log fire.

'Is it that time already?' Abbie got up off the floor, pushing back those loose tendrils of dark hair before reaching out to grasp Charlie's hand and pull her up beside her.

Charlie looked as adorable as her mother, enchantingly so in a knee-length nightgown with a rabbit pattern adorning its front. 'Jarrett!' she cried out excitedly as she ran lightly across the room to hug him, her face glowing from the time of play with her mother.

He couldn't resist the openness with which the little girl greeted him, going down on his haunches to hug her in return—although part of him couldn't help wishing it had been her mother who had been so pleased to see him, and that she had greeted him in the same way!

Dream on, Hunter, he told himself ruefully as he straightened; Abbie was looking at him warily, not with pleasure.

'I'll just take Charlie to bed—' Abbie held out her hand to her daughter '—then I'll change quickly and be with you in a few minutes. I had no idea it was so late.' She shook her head.

Obviously she wasn't exactly filled with anticipation at seeing him again, Jarrett decided. Damn it, he had changed his shirt at least three times, in an effort to strike just the right note, neither too formal nor too casual, finally deciding on a pale lemon shirt with black trousers, unwilling to wear a tie. And Abbie couldn't have forgotten completely that she had invited him here for dinner; after all, the car had been sent for him—although that order, he realised, could have been given hours ago! But she certainly hadn't looked forward to this meeting in the way he had. And the knowledge wasn't exactly flattering to his ego!

'Don't bother to change on my account,' he told her with harsh dismissal. 'You look fine to me as you are.'

She gave him what looked like a scathing glance, his opinion obviously unimportant to her. 'I shouldn't be too long,' she bit out tersely. 'Tony will get you a drink.' She waved a vague hand towards the array of drinks on the side table before leaving the room with Charlie.

Left alone together, the two men eyed each other across the width of the room, Jarrett easily meeting the challenge in the young man's gaze. He hadn't made a good impression on Tony the previous evening, either!

The younger man moved to the drinks. 'What can I get you?'

Jarrett held back his smile at Tony's deliberately bland tone. 'Whisky with ice will be fine, thanks.' He moved to one of the armchairs, sitting down uninvited—if he waited for an invitation from Tony he would be left standing all night. The other man gave the impression he would like to take Jarrett to the top of Whistler Mountain and leave him there—without skis! Again that nagging doubt entered Jarrett's thoughts as to the role Tony might play in Abbie's life... 'Thanks.' He abruptly accepted the glass of whisky Tony handed him.

Tony remained firmly planted in the room. It was impolite to leave a guest to his own devices when he had just arrived, Jarrett accepted that, but he was sure that wasn't the reason Tony remained. He need have no fear of Jarrett stealing the family silver; there was something of infinitely more value, in Jarrett's opinion, that he had his eye on!

Even as he thought of her, Abbie entered the room, having effected a transformation in the ten minutes since she'd left the room, her hair neatly pinned back at her nape, its shining glory totally tamed, her cream blouse neat and uncomplicated, matched with cream fitted trousers that could do nothing to disguise the perfection of her figure. Jarrett was sure her look of cool elegance was meant to put him firmly in his place, but in fact it only made him want to kiss her all the more, to bare her lips of that peach gloss, and make a wild tumble of the dark thickness of her hair.

He reacted like a gauche schoolboy every time he looked at this woman—and it had to stop!

He stood up quickly. 'Amazing—a woman who can get changed in ten minutes!'

Abbie raised dark brows at his mockery. 'And put my daughter to bed,' she reminded him.

She was, he realised, starting to use her daughter as a shield between the two of them, which, rather than evoking the irritation he was supposed to feel, just made him grin. For one thing, he thought Charlie was adorable—and, for another, it showed Abbie felt there was a reason to erect a barrier between them. This woman wasn't as cool towards him as she liked to give the impression she was—as she would obviously like to be!

'Thanks, Tony.' She dismissed the younger man. 'Could you tell Mrs Gregory that we will be ready to eat dinner in ten minutes?'

The blond Adonis didn't look at all happy at being

dismissed in this way, giving Jarrett a look of warning before he left the room.

Jarrett smiled once he and Abbie were finally alone. 'He's obviously taken an instant dislike to me,' he stated uncaringly.

Abbie poured herself a glass of mineral water. 'I'm sure he's far from the first,' she said.

Jarrett's smile didn't waver; in fact it widened. She was no wilting wallflower, this woman, but he liked that about her. In fact, he liked everything about her! 'I'm not out to win any popularity contests.'

'Just as well,' Abbie muttered pointedly, standing across the room—as far away from Jarrett as possible!

He still smiled. 'As arranged, I saw Stephen and Alison this afternoon.'

Her mouth quirked at this. 'And how is Stephen's nose?'

'Unbloodied,' he acknowledged ruefully. 'I thought about what you said,' he explained. 'And decided it wouldn't look too good if Stephen returned from his honeymoon the worse for wear!'

'That was very considerate of you,' Abbie returned dryly.

'Oh, I can be considerate, Abbie,' Jarrett drawled.

She looked at him with chilly violet-blue eyes. 'I believe you have some business you wish to discuss with me?'

Not yet, not if it meant he didn't get to spend the evening with this completely desirable woman. He had a much different end to the evening in mind than being thrown out before he had even eaten!

'It can wait, Abbie,' he dismissed easily.

Her gaze remained steady. 'You gave the impression last night there was some urgency involved.'

He gave a relaxed gesture. 'Having now met you, there's no hurry.' No hurry at all!

This was all very novel for him. Women rarely interested him. Oh, he was as physically attracted to the female sex as the next man, but the actual personalities behind that attraction, the ins and outs of those women's lives, what actually made them tick, had never interested him; in fact, it bored him immensely. But Abbie Sutherland, with her extraordinary beauty, violet-blue eyes, and frosty manner, intrigued him in a way he could never remember a woman doing before.

And, instead of running like hell, he couldn't wait to see the woman again!

Amazing!

But there was so much about Abbie Sutherland that was still a mystery to him. Cathy had given him the impression her stepmother was nothing but a money-grasping opportunist, and yet, faced with the woman herself, for all that it would be better if he could accept that about Abbie, Jarrett was finding it harder and harder to believe. Abbie had a dignity about her, an aloofness that owed nothing to money, and part of him was sure that veneer hid a very vulnerable woman.

Or maybe that was the way she had captured a man like Daniel Sutherland, that aloofness acting as a challenge to him, the vulnerability bringing out the protective instinct in him. Maybe Jarrett was being as gullible as Daniel Sutherland!

His mouth tightened as that possibility occurred to him, and he stood up abruptly, aware that Abbie was now watching him with wary eyes. But making a fool of himself over a woman was something he had sworn would never happen to him. And Abbie Sutherland was not going to prove the exception to that rule!

Her wariness increased as he stepped purposefully towards her, alarm darkening her eyes to pure violet. Almost as if she knew he was about to kiss her!

CHAPTER FIVE

NO MATTER what he might think to the contrary, Jarrett Hunter was not going to kiss her!

Abbie didn't even know why she thought he was going to—there had been nothing in his manner seconds ago to indicate that was his intention—but a part of her was absolutely positive that was exactly what he thought he was going to do. Well, he could think what he damn well pleased; the chances of him actually succeeding were as high as the snow on Whistler Mountain all melting away by morning—nil!

'I don't think so, Jarrett,' she told him sharply as she stepped neatly sideways out of his reaching arms.

He stopped where he was, looking at her with tiger-like intensity. 'No?' he finally drawled.

'No.' She gave a firm shake of her head.

He raised dark brows. 'You aren't attracted to me?'

She blinked at the directness of his question. But it was what she should have expected from this man; he had been totally forthright since the moment she met him last night. In fact, he had been forthright to the point of rudeness!

As for being attracted to him—she wasn't sure what she felt towards him. She knew that since meeting him on the slopes this morning she had found her thoughts wandering from what she was doing several times as she remembered her conversations with him. Which was strange in itself... No man had made such an impact on her, either during her marriage or since it.

She had finally become annoyed with herself, deliberately giving the impression when he arrived earlier that she had forgotten his expected arrival this evening, to such an extent she hadn't even bothered to change. But for all the good that had done as a put-down—if his behaviour now was anything to go by—then she might as well not have bothered!

She met him head-on, betraying none of her inner conflict. 'I have an aversion to being—manhandled,' she told him.

His brows were raised even higher, a seductive smile fleeting across his lips. 'How about if I just kiss you but don't hold you?'

He was deliberately taunting her now. 'In any way, Jarrett,' she bit out harshly.

His stance became relaxed, although he still looked challenging to Abbie. 'I suppose in your position that isn't too difficult to achieve,' he said thoughtfully.

She looked at him with a furrowed brow. 'In my position?' she repeated softly—exactly what had he meant by that?

Jarrett strolled unconcernedly across the room to pick up his glass of whisky before answering her. 'The rich widow of a multimillionaire—I'm sure it can be intimidating to a lot of men.'

It certainly could—and that was the way she liked it! 'Obviously not to you,' she returned.

'That's because I'm a multimillionaire myself,' he told her. 'Besides, Abbie, I'm not easily intimidated.'

She could well believe that, after reading of his disrupted younger years, and the success he had made of his life since that time, despite the odds that were stacked against him doing so. The additional, more personal information she had received on him earlier this afternoon, including the lengthy list of women he was known to have been briefly involved with, did not indicate a man who was easily deterred, either!

Her lips pursed. 'And I'm not into affairs, brief or otherwise!'

He looked unperturbed by the vehemence of her tone. 'Doesn't it get a little lonely there at the top?' he asked, that golden gaze probing.

She couldn't stop the heated colour that entered her cheeks as his barb hit home. God, yes, it was lonely! Much as she loved her daughter, delighted in her company, the evenings and nights that she spent on her own could be very long without someone to share them with. But she wasn't about to admit that to this man!

'It has its compensations,' she countered.

'Such as?' Jarrett raised questioning brows.

Her eyes flashed deeply violet. 'Such as I can do what I like, when I like, and I don't have to answer to anyone else to do it!'

He looked unmoved by her outburst. 'That's an interesting comment, Abbie,' he said slowly.

Her cheeks felt warm again. Why was it interesting? Exactly what implication was Jarrett Hunter reading into her comment that wasn't there?

'Interesting coming from a woman who only yesterday evening,' he continued smoothly, 'informed me she travels all over the world, but doesn't really enjoy it. That doesn't sound like someone who does what she likes, when she likes, and doesn't have to answer to anyone else to do it!' he concluded.

She had known from the first that he was no fool, but, even so, he was far too astute for her comfort! 'Business commitments, Jarrett,' she replied. 'And until Charlie is old enough to take over the reins I have to do it for her.'

'You'll be in your mid-forties by then.'

'Is that relevant?'

'It could be, if you ever intend having a life of your own. A relationship. Other children.'

'I don't,' Abbie snapped. 'Charlie is my life.'

'And when she's grown up, and has a life of her own, what will you have then?'

'What do you have, Jarrett?' She neatly turned the conversation back on him, issuing a challenge of her own now.

'That's different,' he rejoined hardly.

'Why? Because you're a man?' she scorned, shaking her head. 'We're entering a new century, Jarrett, and goodness knows women have come a long way—'

'And pretty soon, with the advances constantly being made in artificial insemination, you won't need men at all!' he finished scathingly.

'I wasn't about to say that,' she told him softly, head back challengingly.

'But it's true, isn't it?' There was a disgusted sneer to those sculptured lips now. 'No doubt women will one day be able to just walk into a clinic, state the sex, hair colour, eye colour, brain power of the child they want, and be able to walk out again knowing they have in their womb exactly what they want. The whole process makes a damned mockery of this love and for ever thing!'

'Then I would have thought it would make perfect sense to you!' she returned heatedly. 'Besides, you're oversimplifying things, Jarrett. That medical process is geared towards couples who find it hard to conceive a child in the normal way—'

'But what I'm suggesting is the next step, isn't it?' he cut in. 'And it takes away all that messy business of "the normal way"!'

Abbie opened her mouth to retaliate. And then closed it again, her face pale, eyes huge and deeply violet.

Jarrett studied her for several long-drawn-out seconds. 'Is that how it was for you, Abbie?' he finally said huskily.

She gave him a startled look, blinking rapidly, knowing that she had briefly—briefly enough for most people not to have even noticed it!—let her guard down as she was flooded with memories of things she would rather forget.

'Was it, Abbie?' Jarrett moved closer, inches away from her now. 'Did you hate making love with your aged husband? Did he repulse you? Did you dread the times—?'

'Stop it!' Abbie flinched, her eyes haunted now, those memories she had pushed from her mind now back with a vengeance. 'Just stop it!' she repeated emotionally.

'Abbie…!' Jarrett groaned in a pained voice, reaching out to clasp her arms and pull her gently into his chest.

Her first instinct was to pull away, but something stopped her, something she couldn't explain; a warmth enveloped her, a warmth she was loath to relinquish. It had been so long since she had known the warmth of another human being beside Charlie. So very long…

'I didn't mean to hurt you.' Jarrett's hands cradled each side of her face as he looked down at her searchingly. 'I would never hurt you, Abbie,' he added before his head lowered and his lips brushed lightly over hers. 'Never, Abbie…!' he ground out, before his lips moved more intently on hers, asking for a response, but not demanding one, his arms light about the slenderness of her waist, as if he knew she would take flight if he behaved any other way.

Abbie responded. Her lips moved slowly against his,

although her hands remained stiffly at her sides. But she didn't feel that driving need to escape, to back off, to run away. This wasn't Daniel, she told herself encouragingly.

But, as if just the thought of her husband had conjured him into the room, she now felt that familiar sense of helplessness, that deep well of emptiness inside her.

She wrenched her mouth away, looking up at Jarrett with disturbed eyes. Jarrett... It was Jarrett. No one else, just Jarrett. But it made no difference, the trembling beginning deep inside her, cold and hot at the same time, her hands shaking as she clasped them together, her breathing shallow and erratic.

'Sit,' Jarrett instructed smoothly, even as he eased her down into one of the armchairs. 'Bend forward. That's it,' he encouraged as she collapsed forward heavily. 'I'll pour you a whisky,' he stated grimly as he moved away.

She swallowed hard, her throat feeling tight. 'I don't drink whisky,' she managed to reply.

'You will now,' he told her firmly. 'It's the only thing I can think of to counteract a panic attack!'

Panic attack...? Was that what this was? God, how stupid, how utterly, utterly stupid. Jarrett Hunter was the one man she should never have allowed near her, and not only had he held her and kissed her, he had witnessed her reaction to those intimacies. And somehow she had to regain her shattered coolness, that barrier that kept all but Charlie at a distance.

She straightened in her chair, flicking back the dark fringe of her hair, forcing an expression of haughtiness to her face as Jarrett returned with the promised reviving alcohol. 'I really don't drink whisky, Jarrett,' she told him evenly as she ignored the glass he held out to her.

He continued to look at her for several long seconds,

and then he lifted the glass and drained the contents himself. 'But I do,' he told her as he placed the empty glass firmly down on the table. 'Now would you like to tell me what the hell all that was about?'

Once again, he was too close, so much so that Abbie could feel the warmth emanating from his body.

She stood up abruptly, moving away from him, relieved to find the trembling in her knees had stopped, her movements quite fluid in the circumstances. 'It wasn't about anything, Jarrett,' she told him with feeling. 'You kissed me. It wasn't to my liking—'

'That's a damned lie!' he cut in swiftly. 'It wasn't me you were frightened of, it was someone else entirely—'

'You're right about one thing, Jarrett: I'm not frightened of you,' she said bravely. 'I just don't like to be—'

'Manhandled!' he finished scathingly. 'I didn't "manhandle" you, Abbie, I kissed you. And you liked it!'

She took a sharp intake of breath, swallowing hard. He was right, she had liked it...

Her mouth twisted into a smile. 'I think your ego may be getting in the way again, Jarrett,' she told him. 'You just can't seem to accept that every female you meet isn't going to fall willingly into your arms!' She was deliberately insulting, knew that at this moment it was her only defence. 'I'll admit I was curious for a while, Jarrett, but—despite what you may have thought—my husband was a more than capable lover. His age, his previous marriage, his years as a bachelor after his first wife died meant that he knew exactly how to please a woman.' Her gaze was coolly steady on Jarrett's now angry face. 'No other man could ever take his place in my life.'

'I don't want to take his place!' Jarrett visibly recoiled. 'You already know my views on marriage—'

'And you already know mine on affairs,' she cut in lightly. 'I believe that brings us to impasse?'

His eyes darkened with annoyance. 'Hell, Abbie, you know I only wanted to—'

'Yes, I believe I know exactly what you wanted, Jarrett.' She was back under control again now, that momentary lapse put firmly behind her. 'And I've told you, quite honestly, that it isn't possible. The only agreement we may come to is on a business level—and even that I find unlikely. Sutherland's isn't in need of a partner any more than I am.'

He didn't look at all happy with her change of subject, scowling darkly, but as business was supposedly the reason he was here at all...! Although Abbie was no longer sure about that, had a distinct feeling Jarrett Hunter had decided to mix business with pleasure. Something Daniel had warned her never to do; emotions were complete anathema to business.

Jarrett recovered with effort, his mouth set in a thin, dissatisfied line. 'Hunter's isn't in need of partners, either,' he finally rasped.

'Then what do you need from Sutherland's?' she returned coolly.

'I don't need—' Jarrett's explosive response was cut short as Tony entered the room after the briefest of knocks.

And Jarrett looked far from pleased at the interruption, glaring at the younger man, Abbie noted before turning enquiringly to her assistant.

'Dinner is ready to be served in the dining-room,' Tony informed her, even as he eyed the other man suspiciously.

Really! Abbie registered the two men's aversion to each other with amusement. One wasn't welcome, the other an employee, and yet they were both acting in a proprietorial manner towards her, treating each other with open disdain. Tony's behaviour she could mainly understand: it was part of his job to protect her. But Jarrett Hunter's behaviour, on so short an acquaintance, especially so volatile an acquaintance, was inexplicable. As well as being inexcusable!

'Thanks, Tony,' she accepted with casual acknowledgement. 'We'll be through in a moment,' she assured him. Although the thought of another couple of hours spent in Jarrett Hunter's disruptive presence wasn't exactly conducive to relaxation!

'He isn't joining us, is he?' Jarrett muttered once the two of them were alone again.

If Jarrett weren't here, then the likelihood was that she and Tony would have shared their evening meal together, but they usually discussed business as they ate, and it wouldn't have been the proper dinner she had ordered to be prepared for this evening, but would have consisted of a snack that wouldn't interfere with the business they were working on.

She looked at Jarrett. 'Would it bother you if he were?' What a stupid question; resentment emanated from every arrogant pore of his body every time he so much as looked at the younger man!

Maybe he still half believed that assumption he had made initially concerning Tony and herself—with a few modifications, of course!

'No, of course he isn't joining us,' she told Jarrett impatiently as he continued to glare. 'Why should he?'

'He seems to go everywhere else that you do,' he observed scornfully.

'Not everywhere, Jarrett,' she disagreed. 'And

minutes ago you were implying my life was a lonely one,' she reminded him tauntingly.

'There's a vast difference between paying someone to be there and having someone there by choice!' Jarrett rasped.

Her cheeks became inflamed at his remark. 'Tony's conditions of employment are very specific, Jarrett,' she bit out. 'And they do not include keeping me happy in bed!' Her eyes flashed deeply violet.

'I'm already aware of that,' he drawled mockingly.

'Oh?' she prompted defensively.

'Mm,' he confirmed with a smile. 'Or, if they do, then he's failing in his duty,' he added. 'You don't have the look of a woman who is kept satisfied in bed!'

Her indignant gasp was purely involuntary; she was rendered temporarily speechless by this man's sheer audacity. No one had ever spoken to her in this insultingly familiar way before! Not even—

'May I point out, Mr Hunter,' she replied caustically, 'that you were the one to seek out this meeting?' There were bright spots of angry colour in her cheeks now. 'Unfortunately, I am going to be the one to end it. I can see no purpose in continuing this conversation between us, find it—and you!—completely insulting! I would like you to leave now,' she told him with quiet dignity, her head held high. 'I will obviously not say anything to Alison and Stephen about the abruptness of this meeting, but—'

'Why "obviously", Abbie?' Jarrett drawled, completely unmoved by her outburst. In fact, if anything, he looked amused by it!

She shot him a furious glance. 'They're friends of yours—'

'And yours,' he put in, his eyes glowing golden with laughter—at her expense!

Her mouth tightened. 'I'm trying to point out that I won't let this affect your years of friendship with Stephen—'

'"This"?' Jarrett taunted softly.

She drew in a harshly ragged breath. 'You are being deliberately annoying, Jarrett—'

'Not deliberately, Abbie.' He shook his head, his gaze warm on her flushed face. 'Where you're concerned I really don't need to try! Why do you think that is, Abbie?' he prompted huskily.

'Oh, please!' she muttered impatiently. 'You're right, Jarrett—you don't need to try! You're nothing but a pain in the—'

'Tut, tut, tut,' he cut in. 'There is a child in the house, you know.'

'I do know,' she snapped at him. 'And I was about to say "rear"!'

'Of course you were,' Jarrett soothed.

'Don't patronise me, Jarrett!' She was becoming infuriated by his calm mockery.

'Okay, I won't.' He folded his arms across the broad width of his chest, eyes dancing with amusement—at her expense!

'You're still doing it!' Her hands were clenched into fists at her sides in an effort to stop herself from actually hitting him.

He shrugged. 'One of the advantages of having two younger brothers. If you think I'm annoying, then you should meet Jonathan and Jordan. I know.' He grimaced at Abbie's raised brows. 'My mother thought it would be amusing to name her sons so that they all had the same initial.'

The mother who had walked out on them all when
her husband went bankrupt… Abbie couldn't help wondering what she felt about them all now, especially her
eldest son, who had made such a financial success of his
life, at least…

'That must have been interesting on Valentine's Day,'
she returned almost humorously, her anger starting to
recede now.

'Not really.'

Abbie snorted. 'I suppose the cards were all for you!'

'Jonathan, actually,' he returned. 'He's the good-
looking one in the family.'

More good-looking than Jarrett? She found that hard
to believe! Although he wasn't good-looking in the full
sense of the word, had a power and forcefulness to his
personality that added to his attraction. He—

What on earth was she doing? She remonstrated with
herself. There was nothing about Jarrett Hunter she
found in the least attractive. Absolutely nothing!

'Is he unmarried too?' she probed.

'We all are.' Jarrett's eyes had narrowed to tawny
slits. 'Our home life as children wasn't conducive to
developing trust in the fairer sex,' he explained harshly.
'In fact, it's probably debatable whether we share the
same father or not!' His amusement had completely gone
now, his expression grim.

Abbie was at once contrite, knowing as she did, from
the information she had been sent on him, a little of his
family background. His mother, by all accounts, had
been far from faithful in her marriage, and in the end
had betrayed both her husband and three sons by walking out on them when the going got too tough.

Oh, no—she couldn't start to actually feel sorry for

Jarrett! That would be positively the worst thing she could do. And he wouldn't thank her for it, either—

'Don't feel sorry for me, Abbie.' He seemed to read her thoughts. 'My mother probably did us all a favour when she walked away from her marriage and us!'

'I—'

'Abbie.' Tony had entered after another brief knock. 'Mrs Gregory says the dinner is spoiling,' he said apologetically.

Dinner... In the continued exchange with Jarrett, she had totally forgotten they had been about to go and eat.

And that, minutes ago, she had asked this man to leave...

She looked across at Jarrett with narrowed eyes. Had he deliberately diverted the conversation for that very reason? Had he hoped to so disconcert her that in the heat of the moment she would forget he had previously insulted her enough for her to ask him to leave?

As she met the challenge in those golden eyes, she knew that was exactly what he had hoped for...!

CHAPTER SIX

She was too astute by half, this gloriously beautiful woman, Jarrett decided with a twinge of regret. He had hoped she would forget asking him to leave, but he could see by the purposeful light in her eyes that he hadn't succeeded in diverting her at all. Damn!

But he had been enjoying himself immensely, he realised with some surprise. Abbie Sutherland was an intensely satisfying woman—and he hadn't even gone to bed with her yet!

He intended to, though. Oh, yes, he definitely intended to make love to this woman. He planned a long and sensual night in bed with her—long enough to make her forget her more-than-capable-as-a-lover-husband!

It had felt like a knife being thrust into his gut, and slowly twisted, when she'd made that comment about her marriage. He had never felt jealousy before, had no real knowledge of what it felt like, but he had known at that moment such a blinding rage it was probably as well Daniel Sutherland was dead!

What was she going to do now? Would she go through with the dinner as planned, or would she throw him out as she had wanted to do minutes ago? He hoped it wasn't the latter. Although this was turning out to be more complicated than he had imagined. Meet the woman—at last!—put the business proposition to her, and get out. That was the way it should have been, the way he had always played it in the past, but if he did that where Abbie was concerned he would probably never see her again And, at this moment, he wanted more than anything to carry on seeing her...

A silence was stretching before them, the narrow-eyed Adonis standing in the doorway watching their wordless battle of wills. Ready to throw him out, Jarrett didn't doubt, if Abbie so much as arched an eyebrow to indicate that was what she wanted.

Jarrett decided to take matters into his own hands. 'I, for one, am starving,' he announced lightly. 'How about you, Abbie?'

She met his gaze, amusement flickering in those violet-blue depths.

Because she knew damn well she only had to say the word, and he would be kicked out of here so fast he wouldn't know what had hit him! His level gaze silently dared her to say that word...

'Starving,' she agreed before turning to Tony. 'Would you tell Mrs Gregory we're on our way right now?'

Jarrett felt his breath leave him in a relieved sigh. Then he felt irritated with himself for wanting her so much. She was just a woman, for goodness' sake; she had the same body as millions of others. Once he had made love to her the mystery would be gone. Once he had made love to her...

She somehow contrived to look utterly feminine in the cream blouse and matching trousers as Jarrett followed her down the hallway to the dining-room, and he couldn't help but admire the graceful movements of her body as she walked. Abbie Sutherland wasn't just any woman, he decided; she was something special, a woman any man would be proud to be seen out with. Perhaps Daniel Sutherland couldn't be blamed for his folly of marrying a woman so much younger than himself, after all; she was the sort of woman you would want complete ownership over...

Which brought him back to the reason Abbie could possibly have married a man so much her senior. Cathy had said she was a gold-digger, and it did seem a possible explanation. So maybe his own business proposal wouldn't be so unwelcome, after all. Then the two of them could drink champagne and go to bed together to celebrate—especially the last!

'How long do you intend staying in Canada, Jarrett?' Abbie asked conversationally as they ate a thick, meaty soup.

He glanced across at her beneath long dark lashes. 'That depends on you, Abbie,' he murmured.

'Me?' She looked startled, and then her creamy brow cleared. 'Oh, you mean because of this business you want to discuss with me.'

No—he meant he had no intention of going anywhere until he had got this woman out of his system! And he could think of only one way to do it... 'Something like that,' he returned enigmatically.

Was that a blush he saw on her cheeks? Did women still do things like that? This one did, he realised incredulously. She was a mystery within a puzzle, a puzzle within an enigma. Not a comfortable combination.

Maybe he should just cut his losses and get out while he could. Maybe— He was behaving like that besotted schoolboy again. This woman controlled a multi-million-pound dynasty, had done so for some time; she was not what she appeared to be at all. He wasn't about to break all of his own rules over someone like her!

'Exactly that,' he qualified hardly, smartly breaking off a piece of bread from the roll on his plate. 'What

I'm proposing, Abbie,' he bit out baldly, 'is that I buy out Sutherland Hotels.'

She stared at him speechlessly, although she seemed to be having a little trouble, he noted, swallowing down the spoonful of soup she had taken into her mouth. The blush to her cheeks owed nothing to embarrassment this time, just as the paleness that quickly followed owed nothing to that emotion either. Abbie Sutherland was clearly stunned at his suggestion!

'I—you—I—' She seemed lost for words when she did finally find her voice.

'Drink some wine, Abbie.' He held out her glass to her. 'I did tell you Hunter's didn't need any partners,' he added as she sipped the wine gratefully. 'And you very badly need to offload Sutherland Hotels.'

She seemed to be ignoring what he was saying, her hand shaking as she drank her wine. And she was going to be angry with herself, Jarrett knew, for even that minor betrayal of the shock she had just received.

She gathered her battered defences together with effort, her expression vaguely contemptuous as she gazed across the width of the table at him. 'I think, Jarrett,' she said slowly, as if to a backward child, 'that you must have been imbibing too strongly before you arrived here this evening!'

Jarrett sat back in his chair, looking at her with open admiration. She was a classy lady. No matter what Cathy might have said to the contrary, no matter what she might or might not have been before she married Daniel Sutherland, she was certainly a first-class lady now. If it hadn't been for that slight tremor in her hands seconds ago...!

'Nice try, Abbie,' he drawled appreciatively. 'Almost perfect, in fact. Almost...'

Her gaze was glacial. 'I have no idea what you're talking about.' She shook her head firmly. 'You told me you wanted to discuss business with me, not tell me jokes!'

Very classy. No wonder Cathy, for all of her private education, finishing-school, and lavish lifestyle, found her stepmother so overwhelming. Abbie Sutherland was the diamond, Cathy the cheap zircona.

Jarrett shrugged. 'I don't see anyone laughing, Abbie.'

'No, I'm sure you don't,' she acknowledged briskly. 'You're being more ridiculous than funny. Sutherland Hotels are amongst the most prestigious in the world, is one of the oldest family-owned groups of hotels in the world; we have hotels in most of the major capitals in the world, plus—'

'Which is why you're running yourself ragged by travelling all over the world, when you obviously would rather not,' he pointed out calmly, his expression remaining bland as she shot him a warning look. 'I've done my homework, Abbie,' he continued. 'Sutherland's is a big corporation; the hotels are only a minor part of it—'

'Sutherland's began with those hotels,' she defended hotly.

'And they've become a yoke around your throat, one that's threatening to choke you,' he returned levelly.

Angry spots of colour brightened her cheeks. 'I don't know where you obtained your information, Jarrett—'

'Reliable sources—Abbie,' he cut in, impressed—but unmoved—by her indignation. He knew what he was talking about, never approached any business deal without being fully informed. Sutherland Hotels were in trouble, so much so they were threatening to bring down the rest of the company with them. He knew it—and so did Abbie...

She put her napkin down on the table, ringing the bell on the wall behind her. 'I'll have these dishes removed, and explain to Mrs Gregory that you had to leave before the main course—'

'Are you asking me to leave again, Abbie?' he drawled mockingly, making no effort to do so. 'If so, you're going for the record—no one has ever had to ask me to leave twice!' he stated, his jaw set in a stubborn line.

'You surprise me,' she countered scathingly, completely in control again now. 'There's a name for people like you, Jarrett,' she continued cuttingly. 'For people who believe they see a company in trouble and decide to make a ridiculous offer—'

'How do you know my offer is ridiculous?' he returned mildly, unmoved by her anger; he had heard it all before, and worse!

Glacial violet-blue eyes swept over him again, full of contempt. 'Isn't it?' she persisted.

'I—' He broke off as the young maid who had brought their soup in earlier appeared in the doorway.

'Could you clear these dishes, please, Clare?' Abbie spoke flatly. 'And ask Mrs Gregory to hold the main course—Mr Hunter is leaving.'

Jarrett didn't falter from observing Abbie's controlled features as the young girl did as instructed. Dinner was definitely over, he realised. Pity. Not because he was interested in the food, but his chances of bedding Abbie—slim though they might have been!—were definitely over too.

'As I said, Jarrett,' Abbie continued once the maid

had departed, standing up abruptly, 'there's a name for people like you—'

'I've heard it,' he replied swiftly. 'Several times, in fact!'

She shook her head again in disgust. 'If I ever decided the time had come to sell Sutherland Hotels—'

'I believe it's when, Abbie, not if,' he cut in.

'You can believe what you like,' she told him. 'Whatever. I certainly wouldn't consider you as a purchaser, no matter what the circumstances!'

He raised dark brows at her vehemence, standing up himself. He didn't doubt she was really rattled by this conversation. Interesting. 'What about your co-partners?' he challenged gently.

She turned back to him slowly, eyes narrowed to steely slits. 'What did you say?'

Jarrett carried on. 'Admittedly you're in control of the principal share, but I believe Catherine Sutherland, and Daniel Sutherland junior, still have a say in the running of the company?' he queried mildly.

Abbie's reaction, however, was far from mild. Her eyes darkened until they looked almost navy, the purple in them blending in with her irises, her cheeks paling to chalk-white, her mouth tightening to a thin line.

Outwardly Jarrett retained his slightly mocking air, but inwardly he was taken aback at the drastic change that had come over Abbie. For all that she looked so angry, he could again see that air of vulnerability that he found so intriguing. Whatever dislike Cathy felt towards Abbie, it was obviously returned—and more!

Abbie swallowed hard. 'You know Cathy and Danny? You've spoken to them?'

Jarrett still watched her, choosing his words carefully. 'I don't actually know them,' he said deliberately. Which was true; he had met both Cathy and Danny, decided they were both extremely shallow individuals, and not worth his attention. 'And they aren't my reliable sources, either, if that's what you're thinking.' He had already known about the problem with Sutherland Hotels long before he'd spoken to either Cathy or Danny; it was his business to know such things!

Some of the tension left Abbie's shoulders, although she still looked far from relaxed, a certain paleness clinging to her cheeks. 'Your sources weren't reliable at all, Jarrett,' she insisted scornfully. 'So you've been wasting your time, chasing after me for months.' She reminded him of last night's conversation with Alison and Stephen. 'Sutherland Hotels are not for sale!'

'Don't be too hasty, Abbie—'

'I'm not being hasty, Jarrett,' she rejoined. 'I'm merely advising you not to waste any more of your time on this. As you've already stated, I control the major share of Sutherland's—'

'On Charlie's behalf,' he amended. 'This isn't about you and me, Abbie—'

'It most certainly isn't!' she confirmed emotionally.

This woman was something else! Okay, he was a cynic, she had even called him a misogynist last night, but as far as he was aware he had never left a woman with any false expectations, had always chosen his relationships carefully for just that reason. That Abbie held him in contempt he didn't doubt, and it infuriated him to the point where he couldn't think straight.

She was cold as ice cream, he had decided yesterday evening without even being aware that Abbie was Sabina Sutherland—but Abbie had done little, since he had become aware of her true identity, to allay that description!

But ice melted, didn't it...? And he had taken enough of her contempt over the last twenty-four hours!

'But it could be, Abbie,' he grated, reaching out to pull her roughly into his arms. 'In fact,' he added harshly, 'I think it already is!'

She stood stiffly in his arms. 'Let me go, Jarrett,' she ordered.

'Not this time, Abbie,' he told her determinedly, arms tightening like steel bands about her slenderness.

She was so thin he felt as if he might crush her. Or break her in two. He didn't want to do either of those things to this beautiful woman. He wanted to hold her, to make love to her—

Hell, he had to make love to her, had been wanting this since the first moment he set eyes on her!

'Abbie!' he groaned low in his throat before his head lowered and his mouth claimed hers.

Her skin was like satin as he restlessly caressed her face and neck with his hands, wanting closer contact with her, wanting full contact with her.

The thought of her naked in his arms sent him spiralling out of control, bending Abbie to his will, wanting her to want him too. She had to want him. He would go quietly out of his mind if he didn't soon make love to her.

Her hair tumbled loosely down her back now, wild and free, and Jarrett wanted that hair wrapped about him. Her touch would feel like velvet, and those wonderful long legs of hers would be entwined about him, her face alight with pleasure as he took them both to heights they'd never known before, her violet-blue eyes dark with excitement, the—

Abbie had gone limp in his arms!

He had been so aroused, so lost in the touch and smell of her, that he hadn't realised, hadn't known—

He looked down at her worriedly. Her eyes were closed, her breathing erratic; she was still motionless in his arms, and yet he was sure she hadn't actually fainted, that somehow she had just retreated to a world where he couldn't touch her...

As her lashes fluttered open he was sure of it, those eyes totally blank of emotion as she looked up at him.

And that was worse than anything she had ever said to him, the lack of life in her eyes twisting like a knife in his stomach.

'Abbie, what—?'

'Jarrett, just go. Please,' she told him flatly. 'The car is waiting for you outside—'

'Damn the car!' he burst out explosively. 'Abbie, talk to me! Tell me what—'

'Three times surely says it all, Jarrett.' She gave the ghost of a smile.

She was referring to the fact that she had asked him to leave that many times...

It did say it all, he agreed, and yet earlier he'd also been sure that briefly—oh, so briefly!—she had actually responded to him.

He drew in a ragged breath. 'I know I've bungled things,' he acknowledged. 'I just—'

'There was nothing to bungle, Jarrett.' She gave a dismissive, vague wave of her hand. 'And there's nothing more to be said.'

There was nothing more to say. Nothing he had to say that this woman wanted to hear. He had never felt so impotent in his life, didn't want to leave, but at the same time knew he had no choice in the matter...

He slowly released her, sighing heavily as the warmth

and softness of her left him. He felt chilled suddenly, that coldness seeming to creep right into his bones.

Almost as if he would never feel warm again. Which was ridiculous. The car he would be driven in would be heated, as was the hotel, and yet he knew it wasn't that sort of warmth that had gone...

Abbie Sutherland had lit a fire inside him, and now she had extinguished it again.

What ever did that mean?

Jarrett's lips thinned as he pushed those disturbing thoughts to the back of his mind. 'I won't say goodbye, Abbie—'

'I should,' she bit back. 'And if you do need to contact me again, for anything, it may be better if you sent one of your brothers to talk to me.'

Not Jonathan! He wasn't allowing that smooth-talking charmer, with his blatant good looks, anywhere near Abbie. He would forgo any interest he might have in Sutherland Hotels rather than do that. He would end up killing Jonathan if he so much as—

Good God, he was jealous!

Jonathan and Abbie hadn't even met each other, and he was having murderous thoughts about his own brother!

He and Jonathan had never clashed over a woman, had made it a rule never to allow any woman to interfere in their family or working relationship. And so far that had never happened. But Abbie was different...

'We'll see,' he returned enigmatically, his mouth twisting wryly. 'I won't thank you for dinner—because my stomach is telling me quite strongly that it hasn't eaten its fill!' Which was actually a lie; he very rarely felt hunger, had no real interest in food except as a fuel to get him through the day, and usually even then

Jonathan or Jordan had to remind him to eat! 'I'll see myself out,' he suggested.

She nodded, not even looking at him.

'Take care, Abbie,' he said softly and, receiving no reply, he let himself out.

Tim was no more friendly on the drive back to the hotel than he had been on the journey here, and, aware that his own evening had been far from successful, Jarrett wasn't in any mood for idle conversation either!

But neither was he in the mood of anticipation he had been in earlier. The evening hadn't gone at all as he had planned it would, either personally or on a business level, and so by the time he arrived back at the hotel he was scowling darkly, going straight through to the bar to order himself a large whisky. After the frustrating end to the evening he had just had, two or three more would make up for not eating a complete dinner!

'Drowning your sorrows?' queried an amused voice when Jarrett was halfway down his second double.

He turned to face Stephen, still scowling as the other man grinned at him. 'What makes you think that?' Jarrett returned guardedly; surely Abbie hadn't already been on the telephone to Alison? No, he somehow didn't think so...

Stephen gave a pointed look at his watch. 'Dinner seven-thirty for eight, and it's still only nine-thirty?' He raised his brows pointedly. 'Cinders is home extremely early!'

'How the hell do you know I went out to dinner at all, let alone what time?' He certainly hadn't mentioned it when he'd seen Stephen this afternoon!

'Alison had a chat with Abbie earlier.' Stephen made himself comfortable on the bar stool next to Jarrett's, at the same time indicating for the barman to provide them with two more double whiskies. 'She happened to mention it.'

Further proof that Abbie hadn't forgotten his expected arrival this evening at all! Abbie had been playing games with him—but he had the distinct feeling neither of them had won! In fact, he knew damn well they hadn't!

'Actually—' Stephen seemed to speak with deliberate casualness '—Abbie is the reason I'm here.'

Jarrett's mouth twisted ruefully. 'And I thought it was my scintillating company you wanted!'

Stephen gave him a reproving look. 'Save the cynicism for the ladies, Jarrett,' he said quietly. 'I've known you too long to be impressed by it. Or convinced.'

Jarrett sat more upright to look at the other man. 'It's a little late in the evening to warn me off Abbie,' he pointed out dryly. 'And why aren't you with Alison? This is the last night of your honeymoon. Don't tell me the two of you have argued this early in your marriage?'

'I told you to cut the cynicism, Jarrett,' Stephen bit out curtly. 'Alison and I haven't argued, and she knows exactly where I am. And who I'm with. I asked Reception to call me when you returned to the hotel,' he explained.

Jarrett looked surprised. 'Did you, indeed? Might I ask why?'

'Because I want to talk to you, of course,' Stephen told him impatiently.

'About Abbie?' he said slowly. This was a bit of a turnaround after Stephen's previous reticence…!

'Yes…' his friend confirmed. 'Alison and I talked it over, and decided you should at least be aware of some of the problems Abbie has encountered in the last couple of years. The reason she—as you put it last night—

doesn't even stay at her own hotels.' Stephen looked grim.

Jarrett eyed him guardedly. 'Yes?'

'Your meeting with Abbie didn't go well this evening?' The other man still looked serious.

'What do you think? No, it didn't go well, Stephen,' Jarrett bit out caustically as his friend looked at him reprovingly. 'In fact, I have the distinct impression Abbie never wants to set eyes on me again!'

'Hmm,' Stephen said consideringly. 'Then perhaps we don't need to have this conversation at all—'

'You and Alison have "talked it over", remember. I said Abbie doesn't want to see me again—but I very much want to see her! And maybe if I knew a bit more about what makes her tick I wouldn't keep walking in there like a bull in a china shop!'

'Maybe,' Stephen agreed with obvious scepticism. 'It's your style, Jarrett,' he explained at Jarrett's narrow-eyed look. 'I—Abbie had a rough time of it after her husband died.'

At least he was beginning to understand! Jarrett inwardly sighed his relief. Anything he could learn about the elusive Abbie had to be helpful.

'Being widowed at—what, twenty-five?—can't have been easy,' he prompted quietly.

Stephen nodded. 'Even less so, surprisingly, when you're the widow of a man like Daniel Sutherland. He—wasn't an easy man, by any stretch of the imagination.' Stephen grimaced. 'But one thing in his favour—he did dote on Charlie.'

'Which is why, presumably, he left her the lion's share of Sutherland's,' Jarrett concluded.

'You know about that?' Stephen watched as Jarrett nodded in confirmation. 'Well, then, perhaps that makes this all the easier to tell. That old saying "where there's a will there's a relative" was all too true in this case. In fact, there were two relatives,' he explained grimly.

'Catherine. And Daniel junior,' Jarrett acknowledged carefully, not wanting anything he said, or did, to stop Stephen now that he had started talking.

Stephen gave him a thoughtful look. 'You know about them, too?'

Jarrett shrugged. 'This was business, Stephen; of course I know of all the parties involved.' But he said nothing of those tedious dinners he'd had with Cathy Sutherland, or the couple of occasions when he had met her brother—and felt like punching the spoilt little wimp on the nose! Danny Sutherland was too busy whingeing about what he hadn't got to be content with the privileged lifestyle that had been handed to him on a plate. He and his sister Cathy were everything that Jarrett despised; they had so much, but they still wanted more.

'Do you also know of the wrangle that went on between Abbie, as Charlie's mother and guardian, and Daniel Sutherland's older children from his first marriage, after the old man had died?' Stephen's expression betrayed his distaste.

Cathy hadn't mentioned anything like that... 'What sort of wrangle?' Jarrett prompted. 'As far as I'm aware, Daniel Sutherland was completely sane when he died, so what was their problem? No doubt the two older children were a bit put out that Charlie was favoured in the way she was, but Daniel Sutherland didn't have to leave them anything at all if he chose not to.' Considering what pampered brats the two older Sutherland children were, Jarrett knew exactly what he would have done in Daniel Sutherland's shoes!

Stephen eyed him steadily. 'What I'm about to tell

NO RISK, NO OBLIGATION TO BUY...NOW OR EVER!

GUARANTEED

PLAY "ROLL A DOUBLE" AND YOU GET FREE GIFTS! HERE'S HOW TO PLAY:

1. Peel off label from front cover. Place it in space provided at right. With a coin, carefully scratch off the silver dice. Then check the claim chart to see what we have for you – TWO FREE BOOKS and a mystery gift – ALL YOURS! ALL FREE!

2. Send back this card and you'll receive brand-new Harlequin Presents® novels. These books have a cover price of $3.75 each in the U.S. and $4.25 each in Canada, but they are yours to keep absolutely free.

3. There's no catch. You're under no obligation to buy anything. We charge nothing – ZERO – for your first shipment. And you don't have to make any minimum number of purchases – not even one!

4. The fact is, thousands of readers enjoy receiving books by mail from the Harlequin Reader Service®. They like the convenience of home delivery...they like getting the best new novels BEFORE they're available in stores...and they love our discount prices!

5. We hope that after receiving your free books you'll want to remain a subscriber. But the choice is yours – to continue or cancel any time at all! So why not take us up on our invitation, with no risk of any kind. You'll be glad you did!

The Harlequin Reader Service® — Here's how it works:

Accepting your 2 free books and mystery gift places you under no obligation to buy anything. You may keep the books and gift and return the shipping statement marked "cancel." If you do not cancel, about a month later we'll send you 6 additional novels and bill you just $3.12 each in the U.S., or $3.49 each in Canada, plus 25¢ delivery per book and applicable taxes if any.* That's the complete price and — compared to the cover price of $3.75 in the U.S. and $4.25 in Canada — it's quite a bargain! You may cancel at any time, but if you choose to continue, every month we'll send you 6 more books, which you may either purchase at the discount price or return to us and cancel your subscription.

*Terms and prices subject to change without notice. Sales tax applicable in N.Y. Canadian residents will be charged applicable provincial taxes and GST.

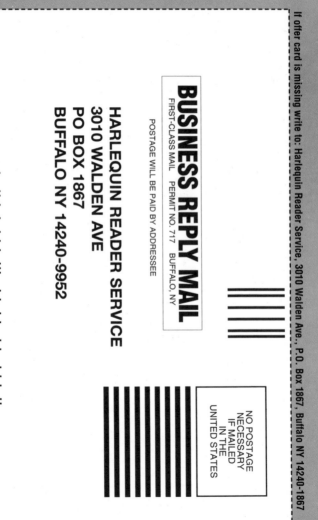

If offer card is missing write to: Harlequin Reader Service, 3010 Walden Ave., P.O. Box 1867, Buffalo NY 14240-1867

BUSINESS REPLY MAIL
FIRST-CLASS MAIL   PERMIT NO. 717   BUFFALO, NY

POSTAGE WILL BE PAID BY ADDRESSEE

HARLEQUIN READER SERVICE
3010 WALDEN AVE
PO BOX 1867
BUFFALO NY 14240-9952

NO POSTAGE
NECESSARY
IF MAILED
IN THE
UNITED STATES

you isn't public knowledge, and I wouldn't be telling you now if I didn't think it important that you know—'

'Well, for God's sake spit it out!' Jarrett rasped impatiently. 'You never used to be a waffler like this, Stephen—'

'And I'm still not!' his friend returned as impatiently. 'I am, however, very fond of Abbie—and no wisecracks about that, please, Jarrett. I appreciate you don't understand words like female friend, or platonic—'

'Patience isn't in my vocabulary, either, Stephen,' Jarrett grated; he was going to shake the information out of the other man in a minute!

Stephen sighed, glaring at Jarrett. 'Catherine and Daniel junior had no intention of trying to prove their father was insane when he wrote his will; they were much more clever than that.'

Jarrett's brow creased. 'I still don't—'

'They approached it from a completely different angle.' Stephen looked grimmer than ever now. 'They set about trying to prove that Abbie was an unfit mother for Charlie, and so equally unfit to be in control of Charlie's share of the company until she was twenty-one. They applied for joint custody of Charlie,' he rasped furiously. 'With the idea that once they had guardianship of Charlie they also had control of her shares of Sutherland's!'

Jarrett stared at the other man. He couldn't be serious. Take Charlie away from Abbie…!

'They didn't succeed, of course,' Stephen continued. 'But, coming so quickly after Daniel's death, it shook Abbie up very badly. She adores Charlie, always has. She never left Charlie before, but now she's even more wary of doing so, even employs people to make sure Charlie is never at risk.'

Jarrett had seen yesterday how much Abbie loved her daughter, and how much Charlie loved her mother, couldn't believe Cathy and Danny had tried to take Charlie from her. But he understood now exactly why Abbie had reacted the way she had when her two step-children had entered their conversation earlier tonight.

He felt rage building up inside him. Those two useless bits of humanity had thought they could take Abbie's daughter away from her—!

He had met those two useless bits of humanity, had dinner several times with Cathy…!

And he had told Abbie he didn't know them…

What the hell was she going to think—of him—if she ever found out how economical he had been with the truth…?

Hell!

CHAPTER SEVEN

'I THINK it's time for bed for both of us, don't you, Charlie?' Abbie prompted her fractious daughter, relieved when Charlie allowed herself to be put to bed without too much of a fight. After the day Abbie had just had she wasn't sure she could have coped with Charlie being difficult now!

No matter how comfortable the plane, it had still been a long flight back from Canada to England, made all the more difficult because Charlie was upset at having her skiing holiday cut short. Usually the most amenable of children, Charlie had proved uncharacteristically uncooperative during the whole journey. Abbie, her nerves already strung out to breaking point, had found it all just too much on top of everything else.

Her decision to leave Whistler had been a sudden one—made about ten minutes after Jarrett Hunter had left the ski-lodge!

He had unnerved her.

The last two years had been far from easy, but with the help of trustworthy people like Tony she had pretty well managed to safeguard Charlie and also her own privacy. A single lapse in that guard—her dinner with Alison and Stephen—had brought Jarrett Hunter into her life. And he was trouble with a capital T!

And he had kissed her...

That was the real reason, if she were honest with herself, why she had left Whistler so abruptly. Usually, she was honest with herself...

She had put off thinking about any of this, had concentrated first on making travel arrangements at such
short notice, and then just getting through the long flight.
Charlie's irritability had helped her to do that; there was
no time to think of anything else when she was trying
to keep her four-year-old daughter amused!

But now, with Charlie safely tucked up in bed, left to
her own thoughts, she knew there was no way she could
stop those disturbing thoughts of Jarrett Hunter intruding.

She sank down into an armchair with a weary groan,
burying her face in her hands. She had realised last night,
when Jarrett Hunter had taken her into his arms, just how
starved of affection and physical warmth she really was.
Far from being repulsed, as she had fully expected to
be, she had hungered for more! She had been stunned
by the realisation. And then she'd panicked. Jarrett, like
every other man she had ever met, wanted something
from her, which didn't involve him giving her anything...

He was what they called a shark in the business world,
watching and waiting for a company that was in trouble,
before moving in for the kill!

How had he found out that Sutherland Hotels were in
trouble, that the luxurious accommodation they supplied
was fast becoming a millstone about the neck of
Sutherland's, and consequently a noose around Abbie's
neck too? She had no idea how he had found out that
information, or how he had known she was rushing all
over the world visiting the various hotels while she tried
to come up with a solution to the problem. A solution
she hadn't yet found. All she seemed able to do at the
moment was hang onto them, for Charlie's sake.

But none of this changed the fact that Jarrett Hunter had kissed her...!

He was everything she despised in a man—cynical, hard, in her opinion a confirmed misogynist—and last night she had just wanted to crawl into his arms and be made love to until she couldn't think straight.

She couldn't have been thinking straight to have wanted that in the first place!

She looked up frowningly as Tony entered the room. He had flown back with her, must be as tired as she was, and yet he had insisted on checking her mail and telephone answering service as soon as they got in, didn't look in the least as if he had just been on a plane for ten hours. Sometimes Abbie felt she was years older than him, felt weighed down by her responsibilities, and yet she knew they were of a similar age.

'Problems?' she prompted with effort, sincerely hoping there weren't any—she just wanted to go to sleep for twelve hours!

He shrugged, looking down at the piece of paper he held in his hand. 'That depends. Jarrett Hunter rang here an hour ago,' he told her stiffly.

She instantly understood Tony's concern; the address of her London home wasn't public knowledge, and the telephone number was unlisted!

'What did he want?' she asked through unsteady lips, too weary to react any further than that. She wasn't even totally surprised; a man like Jarrett could find out anything he chose to—by fair means or foul, but probably foul!

'For you to return his call on this number as soon as you got in.' Tony handed her the piece of paper with a message and telephone number written on it.

His expression was bland, but he was obviously as

curious about their sudden departure from Canada as Charlie was upset. And this telephone call from Jarrett was just adding to his curiosity.

Abbie couldn't meet that curiosity, looking down at the piece of paper, frowning as she did so. It was a London telephone number. How on earth—? Jarrett couldn't be back in London yet; she had only just arrived herself; there was no way he could have got back before her.

The caller had been J. Hunter... But then, as Jarrett had told her, he wasn't the only J. Hunter in his family; both his brothers had that initial too! But she couldn't think why one of Jarrett's brothers would be calling her, either.

Perhaps Jarrett had been involved in an accident? But even if he had been, why would a member of his family be telling her about it? In fact, how had Jarrett known she was back in London at all?

'I'll deal with this,' she told Tony abruptly, crumpling the piece of paper in her hand. 'Anything else of relevance?'

'Nothing urgent.' He shook his head.

She nodded, standing up. 'In that case, I'm going to join Charlie, and go to bed!'

She showered, put on a nightshirt, brushed her hair, drank a cup of tea from the pot that had been brought to her bedroom, but all the time she did these things that piece of crumpled paper seemed to taunt her from where she had put it down on the dressing-table.

What if Jarrett *had* been hurt in some way? It was still nothing to do with her, of course, but by the same token she knew, for all she was exhausted, that she wasn't going to sleep until she had solved the mystery of the telephone call!

'Jordan Hunter speaking,' came the brisk response when the receiver was picked up at the other end.

Not Jonathan, the 'good-looking one in the family'...

'My name is Sabrina Sutherland,' she returned as briskly. 'I believe you called me a short time ago?'

'Abbie!' His voice softened warmly. 'I'm Jarrett's—'

'I know exactly who you are, Mr Hunter,' she cut in coolly. Abbie, indeed! If nothing else, he had at least spoken to Jarrett! 'What was the purpose of your call?'

'Uh-oh,' Jordan Hunter murmured ruefully. 'Jarrett didn't tell me you were mad at him.'

If Jonathan Hunter was the good-looking one, then Jordan Hunter was the one who showed warm good humour, his voice seductive. But if these two men had the looks and the humour, where did that leave Jarrett...?

'I'm not mad at anyone, Mr Hunter—'

'Call me Jordan,' he instantly invited. 'Mr Hunter sounds like Jarrett—and, fond of him as I am, I certainly don't want to be him!'

Jordan had warmth and humour in abundance, Abbie decided as she smiled to herself. 'I suppose that's something in your favour,' she said dryly. 'But that still doesn't tell me why you telephoned me earlier...?'

'You really are that Sabina Sutherland, aren't you?' Jordan said admiringly.

She wasn't quite sure what he meant by that... 'As you already seem to know, most people call me Abbie.' She couldn't help responding to his warmth, or wondering if he looked at all like Jarrett—instantly deciding that even if he did he didn't sound as world-weary and cynical as his older brother! 'How did you get this telephone number, Mr Hunter?' she added firmly, deliberately ignoring his invitation to call him Jordan; she wanted as little to do with this family as possible.

'Jarrett gave it to me,' Jordan supplied unhelpfully.

She sighed her impatience. 'Mr Hunter, I'm tired from my long journey, totally mystified as to your reason for calling me—'

'Jarrett wants to see you,' he put in quickly, seeming to sense she had been about to put an end to the call.

'Jarrett wants to—!' She looked down incredulously at the receiver in her hand, as if it were the instrument itself which offended her, instead of the arrogant Jarrett Hunter. 'In that case, surely it would have been more appropriate if Jarrett had made this call himself?' she returned crossly.

'You are mad at him,' Jordan realised with obvious enjoyment. 'Forgive me, Abbie,' he added hastily. 'It's just a novel experience for a woman to be angry with Jarrett; we usually have to beat them away from his door with a stick!'

So Jarrett did have something! Of course he had something, she instantly berated herself. She had felt that something herself last night. And what he had was so much more lethal than good looks or warm good humour!

'How interesting,' she said sarcastically. 'Exactly what did Jarrett tell you about me?'

'Just that I was to set up a meeting between the two o' you—'

'Again, if he had this number, I still don't see why he had to involve you,' she put in with barely concealed annoyance.

'At this present moment he's somewhere over the Atlantic,' Jordan explained to her. 'Spitting fire and breathing flames. He called me before he left, told me to set up a meeting with you. And when Jarrett is in that mood you don't ask questions like why!' His grimace could be heard in his voice.

Jarrett was following her back to London, was even now on a plane bound for England!

'I see,' she said, her tone measured. 'Well, when he gets back, I suggest you tell him the two of us have nothing further to discuss—'

'I can't tell him that!' Jordan interrupted in protest. 'Have a heart, Abbie,' he went on pleadingly. 'Think of my poor children!'

'I believe Jarrett told me you aren't married?'

'I'm not,' he instantly confirmed. 'But I'm likely to remain childless too if I greet Jarrett with the message you just gave me!'

He painted such a graphic picture that Abbie couldn't hold back her chuckle. 'How about if I agree to a meeting with you instead of Jarrett?' she compromised lightly, her curiosity piqued.

'Same result, I'm afraid,' Jordan sighed. 'Personally, I can think of nothing I would like better than to meet the woman who has my big brother so stressed. But ever fearful of my future prospects as a father…!'

'Okay, okay,' Abbie conceded with a laugh. 'Ten-thirty tomorrow morning, at my office. I'm sure Jarrett knows where that is—he seems to know everything else about me!'

'You can be godmother to my first child!'' Jordan promised with obvious gratitude.

'I agree to the meeting,' Abbie continued firmly, 'on condition that you accompany Jarrett.'

'Oh, I would love to,' Jordan assured her with obvious relish. 'Although I'm not so sure about Jarrett…'

'That's the condition, Jordan,' she told him evenly. 'Take it or leave it.'

'We'll take it,' he accepted hastily.

'Ever conscious of your future prospects as a father…?' Abbie returned teasingly.

'Ever conscious,' he replied. 'And, Abbie… I'm looking forward to meeting you tomorrow,' he added before ringing off.

Charm in abundance, she acknowledged as she replaced her own receiver. From never wanting to see Jarrett Hunter again, she had now been bamboozled—humorously cajoled!—into seeing not just Jarrett but his younger brother Jordan too!

She should have told him to bring Jonathan along too; then she could have met the whole family!

The three Hunter brothers in one room was just too much.

For any woman.

Including Abbie.

'As you seemed so interested in meeting Jordan, I thought I might as well bring Jonathan along to meet you too!' Jarrett told her unapologetically as he faced her across the width of her office, flanked on either side by his two brothers.

Abbie had been left dumbstruck when the Mr Hunters, whom, her secretary had told her were waiting to see her, had turned out to be all three of them!

She had no doubt that Jarrett had neatly turned the tables on her. He stood so tall and imposing in the centre, showing no ill effects from his long flight from Canada the previous night. To the left of him was a man equally tall, obviously younger, with dark curling hair and golden eyes that sparkled with devilment. Jordan. Abbie had no difficulty in identifying him. And to the right of Jarrett stood Jonathan Hunter, again as tall, and with those intriguing golden-coloured eyes, but far more debonair than his brothers in his tailored suit and hand-made shoes, with the sort of blond good looks that threw Tony's handsomeness into the shade. The good-looking member of the family...

Singly, each of these men was too attractive for any woman's peace of mind, but as a trio...! They ought to have some sort of warning attached to them, reading something like, 'Danger: highly explosive!'

'I do believe we've managed to render Abbie speech-less,' Jarrett drawled, stepping forward to break the tab-leau.

Abbie blinked, shaking her head slightly—to clear her brain mainly, although it looked like a denial of Jarrett's claim. 'Not at all, Jarrett,' she returned smoothly, pleased when she heard her voice sound quite normal. She stood up to move gracefully around her desk, tall and slender in a grey fitted suit and contrasting black blouse, her hair secured at her nape. 'Future prospects still intact, I hope, Jordan?' She smiled as she held out her hand in greeting to the youngest man.

He grinned, looking more devilishly attractive than ever. 'Still intact, Abbie,' he confirmed happily before releasing her hand.

She turned to the blond-haired man. 'And by the pro-cess of elimination you have to be Jonathan.' Again she held out her hand in greeting.

'Jarrett didn't tell us how beautiful you are,' Jonathan opined, holding her hand for a fraction longer than was strictly necessary.

But only fractionally, Abbie realised; both the younger men were conscious of the ever watchful gaze of their older brother.

She turned back to Jarrett with playful eyes. 'I would

love to know exactly what Jarrett did tell you about me,' she mused.

'Obviously not much,' he rasped before either of his brothers could reply. 'This is a business meeting, Abbie—'

'Is it?' She arched dark brows questioningly. 'You didn't tell me that, Jordan,' she reproved lightly.

The youngest man shrugged. 'I didn't know. Jarrett likes to play things pretty close to his chest—'

'Jordan!' Jarrett snapped.

Jordan gave another unconcerned shrug in Jarrett's direction. 'I stand corrected,' he muttered with an unrepentant expression on his face.

Jarrett's golden gaze returned to Abbie with narrowed assessment. 'Is it really necessary for these two to be here?' he demanded.

She opened her eyes wide. 'I believe it was your decision to bring Jonathan?' Obviously it was a decision he now regretted, both his brothers were such dominant characters in their own right, Jarrett's attempt to wrongfoot her by bringing Jonathan along, as he believed she had him by requesting that Jordan accompany him, obviously having backfired on him. These two men might be slightly in awe of their older brother—although so far Jonathan had given no indication of it!—but they certainly weren't cowed by him.

'Actually,' Jonathan put in, 'I thought I might come along to see what all the fuss was about. Jordan has done nothing but sing your praises since speaking to you yesterday,' he explained huskily, honey-coloured eyes openly admiring as he met Abbie's gaze. 'Having now met you, I can see why!' He grinned—instantly dispelling that languidly bored expression with which he normally seemed to view the world; the result was breath-taking!

Abbie found herself smiling back at him—until she happened to glance at Jarrett. His scowl was enough to dampen any enjoyment on her part. He was right; his brothers were a distraction that she, for one, didn't need!

She moved confidently to sit back down in the chair behind her desk. 'I just thought it might be nice to meet at least one of your brothers,' she commented.

'Nice!' Jarrett echoed gratingly. 'I've never heard meeting these two clowns described as "nice"!'

'There's only one clown in this family—and it certainly isn't me!' Jonathan observed, that languidly bored expression firmly back in place as he moved forward to raise Abbie's hand, lightly touching the back of it with his lips. 'I hope we meet again, Abbie,' he said.

'In your dreams, Jonathan!' Jarrett said under his breath.

Jonathan remained unperturbed as he unhurriedly released Abbie's hand, mockingly returning his older brother's glare. 'Chink, chink, Jarrett,' he taunted.

Jordan stepped forward, his eyes alight with that devilment that seemed to be such a part of him, picking up the hand Jonathan had so recently released. 'I don't suppose you would consider being mother rather than godmother?' he suggested hopefully.

Abbie laughed; this man really was irresistible! 'I don't suppose I would,' she refused, but the smile remained on her lips as he continued to grin at her.

'Pity,' he said regretfully. 'Godmother it is, then.' He released her hand.

'What the hell are you wittering on about, Jordan?' Jarrett didn't seem to be able to control his tension a moment longer, every muscle and sinew in his body taut.

'Nothing of any relevance to you,' Jordan returned unhelpfully. 'I think we may as well go, Jonathan; we're obviously not wanted here. By Jarrett, at least,' he added with complete disregard for his oldest brother's glare.

'We'll see you later, then, Jarrett,' Jonathan said.

'Possibly,' Jarrett answered.

'It really was good to meet you, Abbie,' Jonathan paused at the door to say.

'I'll say it was,' Jordan agreed enthusiastically. 'I was intrigued by your voice, but the reality is so much more—'

'Will the two of you just go?' Jarrett barked as he dropped down into the chair that faced Abbie's desk.

Jordan grinned, shooting Abbie a conspiratorial wink before following Jonathan from the room, a wink Abbie couldn't help responding to with yet another smile—a smile that as quickly faded as she turned back to find Jarrett scowling darkly across her desk at her.

He looked ready to commit murder—and she wasn't sure she wasn't the intended victim!

CHAPTER EIGHT

ABBIE had never smiled at him in the way she had just smiled at Jonathan and Jordan!

Dear Lord, he was jealous! So jealous he could actually have punched one—or both!—of his own brothers. He could hardly believe the way he felt towards the two brothers he had helped bring up. And all because Abbie had smiled at them!

Why had she smiled at them?

Okay, so Jordan was a tormenting devil, and Jonathan so good-looking he made statues of Apollo look dull and uninteresting, but that still didn't explain why— Hell, Abbie liked Jordan and Jonathan! But she didn't like him...

He had been made all too aware of that when he'd returned to her ski-lodge yesterday morning and found her gone. His initial reaction, after speaking to Stephen in the bar, had been to go back up the mountain and explain everything to her, but he had decided that was madness, that it was late, and Abbie had probably already gone to bed. So, instead, he had spent a sleepless night planning what he would say to her when he did see her—only to find her gone when he got there! Back to England, the frosty Mrs Gregory had informed him— obviously still feeling slighted by the fact that he hadn't finished eating the meal she had prepared the night before!

Jarrett had been stuck in Canada several hours longer, unable to get booked onto a flight. In desperation he had turned to Jordan—not Jonathan, he had decided even then; he didn't want Jonathan, with his lethal good looks, anywhere near Abbie—only to find that Abbie and Jordan had got on so well during their telephone conversation, she had invited him to come along with Jarrett today! When Jonathan had also expressed an interest in meeting Abbie he had just given up; what did it matter if the whole family ended up besotted with her? She was the Ice Queen, anyway!

But she hadn't been the Ice Queen with Jordan and Jonathan. Only with him...

'Chink, chink', Jonathan had mocked him—and he was right; Abbie was fast becoming the chink in his armour!

He glared across the desk at her. 'Satisfied?' he rasped angrily.

She raised dark brows, coolly meeting his gaze. 'With what?' she bit out in a clipped voice.

He sighed. In fact, he felt so filled with impatience he still wanted to explode. But not in front of Abbie. And he would much rather kiss her than vent his anger on her. But kissing her would be a mistake, too. Look what had happened the last time he kissed her...!

'Why did you leave Canada so hastily, Abbie?' he asked without any further delay.

'Did I?' she returned uncooperatively.

He drew in a controlling breath, damping down his anger. 'It was my understanding you were there for some time,' he said flatly.

'My arrangements are always flexible.'

Especially if she met an intrusive bastard like him, Jarrett easily guessed. 'Stephen and Alison seemed as surprised by your sudden departure as I was; they came back on the same flight as me,' he supplied at her frown.

'Alison and Stephen are used to my unpredictability by now,' she again dismissed.

His mouth twisted with irritation. 'Well, I'm not—'

'How did you get my home telephone number?' she interrupted.

He was taken aback momentarily by her sudden change of subject. 'What?' He blinked.

'My home telephone number—how did you get it?' she repeated in a steady voice. 'Not Alison and Stephen, surely?'

He had the distinct impression that if he said yes Alison and Stephen would never be trusted by Abbie again. But Abbie had no need to worry on that score; the newly married couple had been decidedly unforthcoming, deciding they had already said enough by telling him of the dissent in the Sutherland family after Daniel Sutherland died, both of them refusing point-blank to give him any more information on Abbie.

No, it had been someone else completely who had given him Abbie's home telephone number...

'Reliable sources, Abbie,' he reminded her softly. 'Not so unreliable, after all, hmm?' he couldn't resist adding, starting to relax a little now that the disturbing presence of his brothers had been dealt with.

Although Abbie looked less happy now, her mouth tightening. 'That telephone number has already been changed,' she told him coldly.

His brows arched. 'Rather inconvenient for you,' he drawled.

Her eyes flashed deeply violet. 'No more inconvenient than receiving unwelcome telephone calls,' she snapped back pointedly.

She really was upset about this breach in her privacy,

he realised. And, after the things Stephen had told him, he couldn't exactly blame her...

His expression softened as he looked across at her. So cold and detached. So damned vulnerable...!

'Abbie—'

'What do you want, Jarrett?' she demanded caustically, her patience obviously at an end. 'I have a business to run, a—'

'Where's Charlie today?' he queried mildly.

She looked taken aback by the question, a frown furrowing her brow. 'What do you mean?' She moistened her lips in a nervous gesture.

Jarrett watched the unconscious movement, wishing it were his tongue running over— Stop! He had decided, after talking to Stephen the other evening, that he would back off in that direction, give Abbie some space, time to get to know him. If only she weren't so damned beautiful, and, as he now knew only too well, so *vulnerable*.

'I just wondered what you do with Charlie when you're at work?'

He watched as she smiled at the thought of her daughter. Hell, she smiled at everyone but him!

'I rarely come into the office,' she supplied economically. 'I usually work from home.'

His mouth twisted. 'You decided to make today the exception?' And he knew exactly why; despite what she might have said earlier, Abbie was treating this exactly as a business meeting, had no intention of letting him into her private life, or close to her daughter, ever again!

'Charlie is spending the day with a friend.'

'As compensation for cutting short her skiing holiday?' As he watched the colour creep slowly into Abbie's cheeks he knew that was exactly what had happened. Poor Abbie. For all that Charlie seemed like a sweet child, her disappointment over the abrupt ending of her holiday must have been acute, a disappointment she had no doubt made plain to her mother. And that was his fault too, he was sure. Yet another black mark notched up against him in Abbie's eyes!

'As I said, she's spending the day with a friend,' Abbie repeated evenly. 'Now, what business did you want to discuss? I thought we had covered all that in Canada,' she clipped. 'More than adequately!'

Not as far as he was concerned. He knew Abbie needed to offload Sutherland Hotels—just as he knew she had decided he was the last person she would ever sell them to. He had never allowed personal likes and dislikes into his own business—

'You've spoilt them, you know,' Abbie remarked in an amused voice.

Jarrett stared, momentarily disoriented by the remark. 'Who?' He shook his head in puzzlement.

'Jonathan and Jordan.' She relaxed back in her seat, a smile playing about her lips. 'Although there's no doubting their love and respect for you. Which is as it should be. In the circumstances,' she added softly.

Now it was Jarrett's turn to feel on his guard. Exactly what did this woman know about him and his family? 'Circumstances?' he repeated defensively.

Violet-blue eyes met his narrowed gaze unflinchingly. 'You aren't the only one with reliable sources, Jarrett.'

Which told him precisely nothing! That Abbie had had him checked out he didn't doubt; she probably did that as a matter of course after the problems she'd had two years ago. As long as she hadn't learnt of his meetings with Cathy and Danny! That was the reason he had panicked after speaking to Stephen; Abbie didn't exactly appear as if she and her stepchildren were on speaking terms! Although her agreement to see him today, albeit with Jordan in tow, had reassured him that she had no idea of his acquaintance with Cathy—yet.

But no doubt she had learnt of his varied private life, so it was no wonder she viewed him with distrust!

He decided to take her remark at face value. 'Jonathan and Jordan might seem like a couple of jokers, but they're actually very good at what they do. We make a pretty formidable team!' he told her with satisfaction.

'I'm sure you do,' she returned satirically. 'Jordan teases and cajoles, Jonathan renders them speechless with his lazy charm—and then you move in for the kill!'

He drew in a sharp breath. It wasn't the first time she had levelled that charge at him, and, although it had never bothered him before what other people thought of him, it mattered to him now. 'I'm always fair, Abbie,' he told her. 'I know only too well myself what it's like to be on the receiving end of financial difficulties,' he added without bitterness; things had worked out well for him, so what was the point of regret?

Yes, it had been hard when his father had gone bankrupt and his mother had walked out on them all, but Jarrett knew he had made a success of his life in spite of that, not because of it. And Jonathan and Jordan hadn't suffered too badly because of it; he had made sure of that. And his father, now in his sixties, had finally met someone he was completely happy with, and lived in Australia. From disaster had come success, and if he and his brothers were slightly cynical concerning women, then so be it.

Although his cynicism concerning Abbie had become less so as he had come to know her. Although she was still such a mystery to him. Why had such a young and beautiful woman married a man so much older than herself? Abbie had been a successful model, earning big money by all accounts, so why had she chosen to change her life so drastically? There were so many questions about this woman he wanted answers to—and he knew she wasn't going to be the one to provide them!

'My offer for Sutherland Hotels is a genuine one, Abbie,' he told her briskly. 'Business, pure and simple.'

She studied him warily. 'Why do you want them?'

He replied casually, 'I own hotels all over the world myself—as I'm sure you know,' he explained, sure that she did know. 'Sutherland Hotels are all in prime positions, and with minor modifications they could become viable again.'

'If that's so, why haven't I made those modifications myself?' she said, unconvinced.

He answered, completely unperturbed, 'I don't know—why haven't you? Probably because Sutherland Hotels represent something to you—prestige and exclusivity, to name but two things.'

'And by "minor modifications" I presume you mean to eliminate both those things?' She looked disapproving.

'They wouldn't be Sutherland Hotels any more, Abbie,' he reasoned. 'So it wouldn't affect Sutherland's reputation. Business, Abbie,' he reminded her hardly. 'Put aside your dislike of me, and see what Hunter's have to offer you.'

'You are Hunter's,' she reminded him wryly.

'Principally, yes. But so are Jonathan and Jordan,' he rejoined. 'And you seemed to find them amusing enough.'

Again Abbie smiled at the mention of his brothers. Much to Jarrett's chagrin. If this was jealousy, he thanked heaven he had never felt it before now. It was the most uncomfortable of emotions!

'Probably if I had sent one of them to Canada to talk to you, instead of going myself,' he continued gratingly, 'this would all be settled by now!'

Abbie looked at him with that customary coolness in her violet eyes. 'I find them amusing, Jarrett,' she conceded. 'But no more convincing than you are. Why don't you send the details of your proposed deal to me here, and I'll give them due consideration?' she added with a briskness that smacked of dismissal.

'I can easily tell you the details now—'

'I don't do business that way, Jarrett.' She cut him short. 'I have assistants, people I would need to discuss it with. Plus, as you've already reminded me,' she added tersely, 'I have two business partners who have to be consulted too!'

Which, as far as Jarrett could see, was where the problem really lay. If he told Abbie he had already spoken to Cathy and Danny and they were already in agreement with the sale, then she would probably throw him out without a second thought. But if he didn't tell her, and she found out anyway, the result would be the same.

When he had telephoned Jordan from Canada it had been with only one thought in mind, and that was to reach Abbie before she had any contact with Cathy or Danny. Well, it seemed he had managed to do that, but now what did he do? Business, pure and simple, he had told Abbie, but he had lied... He wanted to know this woman better. Much better...

'You're the guardian of the principal shareholder, Abbie,' he stated flatly. 'Therefore you have the deciding vote.'

'And if it were left to Cathy and Danny the whole of

Sutherland's would be sold off and the money divided!' she told him heatedly.

He was sure she was right; Cathy and Danny hadn't given him the impression they were in the least interested in the business it had taken their father a lifetime to build.

'Wouldn't that be the easiest thing for you, too?' he prompted with caution,.

'I made Daniel a promise before he died, Jarrett.' Her eyes glittered with anger. 'And I don't break my promises.'

She was magnificent when she became emotional like this. How he would love to see her emotional, and naked, in his bed!

'Perhaps it was a little unfair of Daniel to ask you to make such a promise,' he reasoned softly. Although it explained why she pushed herself so hard. A woman of honour—that was a novelty in itself! It also brought back those uneasy feelings he had concerning her; she was the sort of woman he had spent a lifetime avoiding. The sort of woman you found yourself promising for ever to...

'Life itself can be unfair, Jarrett,' she told him distantly. 'All any of us can do is take the cards we're dealt in life and play with them.'

Jarrett looked at her assessingly. She sounded so cynical for one so young. But, hell, he had been cynical by the time he was twenty-seven too—long before he was twenty-seven! It just didn't sound right coming from Abbie...

'Were you happily married, Abbie?' he pressed gently, at once seeing the way she stiffened, her expression once again shuttered down. 'Bear with me, Abbie.' He attempted to cajole her as he could see she was on the point of asking him to leave again. 'I'm the result of a broken home; I'm just curious as to whether there are any happy marriages!'

She relaxed slightly. But only slightly... 'Alison and Stephen are happy,' she said briskly.

'They have only been married two weeks!'

Even Abbie had to smile at that, and Jarrett felt his own tension ease as he looked at the warmth in her eyes. He would give anything to have her smile at him like that again, to be genuinely comfortable in his company.

'Have dinner with me, Abbie,' he burst out instinctively. 'Don't say no without even thinking about it,' he added before she could do exactly that. 'What is wrong with me that you won't even have a meal with me in a public restaurant?' He felt as if he was pleading with her, something he had never done with any woman, but at the same time he wanted to spend time with her.

Her mouth curved into a rueful smile. 'You're cynical. Manipulative. And extremely arrogant.'

He raised dark brows. 'Besides that?'

Abbie gave a husky laugh. 'Pig-headed. Rude. Totally unprincipled.'

He pursed his lips thoughtfully. 'And what about the bad points?'

She laughed again—which was a great improvement on the wary way she usually viewed him. Perhaps he was making progress, after all.

'How about if I promise not to even mention business if you'll spend the evening with me?' he persisted.

'In that case, what would be the purpose of us having dinner together at all?'

'It's called being sociable, Abbie,' he said. 'People do it all the time, I believe.'

He could see by her perplexed expression that she

didn't. What sort of life had she led the last two years to be so sceptical? Stupid question, Jarrett instantly berated herself. She had been dealing with people like Cathy and Danny Sutherland the last two years, that was what she had been doing, fending off people who wanted something from the Sutherland name, or Abbie herself, he would hazard a guess. There were all too many men who, while considering Abbie beautiful, would see the Sutherland millions as being even more attractive than the woman herself.

Well, he had made his views on marriage more than plain, so she couldn't think that of him! Although she did, no doubt, still suspect his motives...

'Do they?' she returned lightly. 'Then perhaps I should try it.'

Jarrett found himself staring at her; was she saying yes to his invitation?

'Would eight o'clock suit you?' she continued in a businesslike fashion. 'I'll leave you to book a table, and then perhaps you could let me know where later today so that I can meet you there?'

Jarrett hadn't moved. He had the feeling he had somehow missed something in the conversation. He just wasn't sure what it was... ''You've changed the telephone number, remember?' he reminded her.

'Of course.' She gave a small smile to herself.

'Never mind,' Jarrett said. 'I'll call for you,' he told her distractedly, still slightly bewildered by her acquiescence.

Her mouth quirked. 'You know the address?' 'I know the address,' he confirmed flatly.

'Fine,' she nodded. 'If there's nothing else...? As I've been away for a few days, there are a few things here that need my attention,' she added pointedly as he made no move to leave.

Jarrett got up, his confusion deepening minutes later, when he found himself in the carpeted corridor outside her office.

He had missed something. He was sure of it. He just couldn't place what it was…

CHAPTER NINE

ABBIE remained sitting in the chair behind her desk, shaking from head to foot, thanking God she had been able to control herself until after Jarrett had left her office. She had thought she wasn't going to be able to, had agreed to have dinner with him tonight only as a means of speeding his departure before her nerves got the better of her.

Had she been happily married to Daniel? Jarrett had asked her.

The marriage had been a nightmare. A living hell. One she had only escaped from on Daniel's death...

She had had to avoid answering Jarrett's question at all costs. Yes, she had accepted a dinner invitation from him as the price for that evasion, but in the circumstances it had been a small price to pay...

It was years since she had got herself ready to go out on a date. Although perhaps this evening couldn't strictly be called a date. But it wasn't a business meeting, either, Jarrett had assured her all too forcibly.

She felt nervous, like a young girl, instead of the widow she was. Ridiculous.

She looked at her reflection in the full-length mirror in her bedroom: the dress was right, blue bordering on violet, an exact match for the colour of her eyes, its high-necked, long-sleeved, fitted style ending discreetly above her knee. Flattering, but at the same time not seductive. Her make-up was light and also discreet, although she could do nothing about the natural high colour in her cheeks, or the sparkle that lit her eyes.

Her hair. She really didn't know what to do with her hair. She preferred it long and flowing down her back, as it was now, but instinct told her to pin it at her nape as she usually did. She looked older, less approachable, with her hair confined, and—

'You look lovely, Mummy.' Charlie stood in the doorway, smiling her pleasure at her mother's appearance.

'Thank you, darling.' Abbie held out her arms to her daughter. 'Have you come to say goodnight?'

'Can I say hello to Jarrett first?' Charlie pleaded wistfully. 'He's just arrived,' she explained. 'I heard a car, and when I looked outside I saw him in the driveway.'

Jarrett was here already! Abbie quickly looked at her slender gold wristwatch: eight o'clock. Jarrett was exactly on time. And now she didn't have time to do anything with her hair even if she had decided she wanted to.

'He looks gorgeous, too, Mummy,' Charlie added excitedly. 'Like the Prince in my story books!'

Jarrett Hunter looking like a prince! Abbie could barely stop herself from laughing at the image that evoked. He certainly wasn't Prince Charming; of that she was certain!

'If you say so, darling.' She humoured her daughter, still smiling. 'And yes, I suppose you can say hello to him. Two minutes!' she warned as Charlie's excitement deepened, knowing she would be lucky if her daughter kept to those two minutes; visitors to the house were few and far between, in fact a rarity. Jarrett Hunter had no idea how privileged he was. Or perhaps he did...

Charlie was skipping with happiness by the time the two of them reached the lounge where Jarrett had been asked to wait, and Abbie found her daughter's pleasure was infectious, finding herself smiling across the room at Jarrett as Charlie almost launched herself into his arms.

For a man who obviously wasn't used to small children he coped very well with Charlie's enthusiasm. And Charlie obviously liked him very much, chatting away to him now about the day she had just spent with her friend Clementine.

Jarrett's gaze met Abbie's over the top of her daughter's head, the two of them sharing a moment of pleasure in the child's spontaneity, Abbie the one to finally look away, finding herself suddenly unnerved by those few moments of intimacy. Charlie had only been two when Daniel died, little more than a baby really, and so there had been few shared moments in her childhood like this one.

Though Jarrett Hunter was not the man to share them with!

'You're doing a wonderful job of bringing her up,' Jarrett straightened to tell her once Charlie had been persuaded to go to bed. 'Charlie is like any other child of four, spontaneous—and, like her mother, utterly charming.'

Abbie stiffened. 'And why shouldn't she be?' she said defensively, ignoring his compliment to her.

Jarrett smiled. 'I was complimenting you, Abbie, not criticising. A lot of four-year-olds in Charlie's privileged position would already be spoilt little brats!'

She gave the ghost of a smile. 'Thankfully, Charlie has no idea yet of her "privileged position".' The only real difference so far in Charlie's young life, when compared with that of any other four-year-old, was that she had someone guarding her at all times. Even today, when she had spent the day with her friend, Tony had been with her. Luckily, Charlie saw nothing odd in that. Yet... 'The admiration seems to be mutual,' she told Jarrett. 'Charlie thinks you look like a prince this evening,' she explained at his questioning look.

To her surprise, Jarrett laughed at the description, a genuine burst of laughter that lightened his eyes to gold, and totally erased his usual cynical expression, at the same time taking years off him. He looked more like the mischievous Jordan at that moment!

'I hope you didn't disillusion her,' Jarrett drawled as he sobered, his eyes still warmly golden.

Abbie shook her head. 'Time enough for disillusionment when she's older,' she replied sadly.

'True,' he acknowledged wryly. 'Did Charlie also tell her mother that she looks like a princess this evening?'

She knew they had agreed not to discuss business this evening, but she wasn't sure having Jarrett flirt with her was a good idea, either! She didn't doubt this man could be positively lethal when he set out to seduce. After all, according to that report on him, he had had plenty of practice!

'Then we'll make a dazzling pair, won't we?' she dismissed briskly, picking up her small evening bag. 'I'm ready to go, if you are.'

He grinned at her businesslike tone. 'Used to making the decisions, aren't you?' he teased as he picked up his car keys.

Not until the last two years, when she had been forced into making decisions that weren't always easy to make. Before that time, Daniel had made all the decisions, for all of them...

She met Jarrett's gaze with her familiar coolness. 'Is that a problem?' He was a decision-maker himself...

'I'll tell you if it gets to be that way.' He lightly clasped her arm. 'I'm not particularly interested in insipid women—or ones that pretend to be that way, until you get to know them better!'

He was a complex man; she must remember that. She also had to remember, despite what had been said earlier, that this man wanted something from her. He could be very charming when he chose to be!

'Is Tony coming with us this evening?' Jarrett asked casually—although Abbie could tell he would be far from happy if the other man did accompany them!

She gave a smile. 'He's spending the evening at home, keeping an eye on Charlie.'

Jarrett quirked dark brows. 'Does that mean I passed the security check?'

'It means—' Abbie met his gaze tauntingly '—that Tony's spending the evening with Charlie.'

'Ever the enigma, Abbie!' he stated.

'Ever the opportunist, Jarrett,' she returned smoothly.

He laughed, opening the door for her, the fact that he made no reply a statement in itself…!

The restaurant he had chosen for them didn't just serve food; a small band was playing and there was a dance floor. Abbie looked longingly at the latter as they sat down at their table; it was years since she had danced. The last two years there hadn't been time, and Daniel hadn't been a man who liked to dance, or to let his wife dance with another man.

'We can dance later, if you would like to.' Jarrett had obviously been watching her interest in the couples already moving around the floor.

She opened her mouth to say yes, she would love to— and then she looked at the man she would be dancing

with. Jarrett was tall and lithe, with an attraction she had
responded to more than once, and if they danced together he would no doubt hold her close against that
litheness... Maybe dancing with Jarrett wasn't such a
good idea!

'I haven't danced for years,' she replied, pretending
an interest in her menu that she didn't feel.

Why should she feel so disappointed that she had decided not to dance? She hadn't really done what she
wanted for years, so why should it matter now?

'But you must be a natural,' Jarrett protested lightly.
'You move so gracefully, anyway,' he went on at her
cautious expression. 'Besides, I chose this particular restaurant for the very fact that we could dance together
later on in the evening.'

Abbie gave him a sharp glance, instantly wary. He
had intended dancing with her all along, had chosen this
restaurant for that very purpose. 'We'll see,' she told him
enigmatically.

Jarrett gave a relaxed smile. 'I'm not Charlie asking
for a treat,' he teased. 'And I don't think dancing can
be classed as manhandling,' he added dryly. 'Besides,
what could I possibly do to you on a public dance floor?'

Hold her. Touch her. Just those two things alone were
enough to cause a shiver of awareness down her spine!

'Shall we order?' she prompted as the waiter appeared
dutifully at their table, Abbie anxious now to get tonight
over and done with. The sooner they ate, the quicker she
would be able to do that.

'Drinks first,' Jarrett told her sociably. 'What will you
have?'

She ordered a sparkling mineral water, while Jarrett
ordered a whisky for himself, determinedly returning to
her menu once they were alone again.

'You could be the one driving us home at this rate,' Jarrett commented a few minutes later after ordering a red wine to go with their meal.

'What makes you think I can drive?' After all, he had never seen her do so.

He smiled confidently. 'Abbie, you can do anything you want to do.'

'I doubt that,' she replied, watching the people around them as they enjoyed themselves.

It seemed so long since she had relaxed like this, experiencing an evening out where she didn't have to be something or someone she would rather not be. Although she knew Jarrett was probably the last man she should feel able to relax with, she couldn't help the sense of well-being that was creeping over her. Jarrett made her feel cared for and protected, while at the same time not attempting to dominate her. A dangerous combination...

'You seem to have charmed both my brothers,' Jarrett told her. 'They both think you're wonderful, have done nothing but talk about you all afternoon,' he added mock-disgustedly.

Remembering that mischievous pair, Abbie could quite believe him; Jonathan and Jordan would have enjoyed playing games with their older brother, had probably had a hilarious afternoon—at Jarrett's expense!

She arched dark brows. 'I'm surprised you managed to get out of the house without them!'

'Give me credit for some sense, Abbie.' He shook his head. 'I live on my own. As do Jonathan and Jordan.'

As an only child, Abbie had never known what it was like to have brothers and sisters, and she supposed, with all three men being in their thirties, that they were a little old still to be living in the same house. Probably working together, on a day-to-day basis, was more than enough. For all of them!

'Do you have any family, Abbie?' Jarrett asked as he seemed partly to read her thoughts. 'Besides Charlie, that is.'

She avoided the probing of his golden gaze. 'Not any more,' she answered evasively.

'Not even parents?'

'Not any more,' she repeated stiffly. Abbie's mother had died while she was still a young child—in fact Abbie barely remembered her—and her father had died three years ago, finally succumbing to cancer. Apart from Charlie, there was no one. And, in view of the twists and turns her life had taken over the years, that was probably for the best.

'I couldn't interest you in a pair of spare brothers, could I?' Jarrett asked with soft derision.

For a moment Abbie looked at him blankly, locked in memories of the past. And then, as Jarrett's words penetrated the vividness of those memories, she found herself laughing. She didn't doubt that, at times, Jonathan and Jordan made his life pretty unbearable. They were probably what also made him human!

'Not the two you're referring to, no,' she refused, laughing still.

'In other words, I'm welcome to them, hmm?' he accepted with humour.

This evening wasn't turning out at all as she had expected—she was actually enjoying herself! And, as the food arrived, and the conversation continued to flow easily, Abbie found herself relaxing totally.

It had been too long since she had felt wanted and appreciated in a man's company, since she had responded to that warm admiration in a man's eyes. And the gold in Jarrett's eyes radiated such warmth...

She was so relaxed, by the company and the wine, that by the time Jarrett asked her to dance at the end of their meal she didn't even hesitate, rising gracefully to her feet to move smoothly into his arms as they stepped onto the dance floor.

Jarrett was a good dancer, fluid and rhythmic, with none of the awkwardness in moving to the music that some men felt. She should have known he would be good; Jarrett could do anything he wanted to do too, and not just well, but excellently!

His hand was comfortable on her back, the fingers of his other hand intertwined with hers, Jarrett's hands long and tanned, Abbie's fingers pale and delicate in his grasp. He was as close as she had known he would be, their bodies fitting perfectly together as they moved in time to the music, Jarrett's aftershave male and subtle.

Abbie swallowed hard as Jarrett gently rested his cheek against her temple, the warmth of his breath stirring her hair.

She was having trouble breathing. And she felt hot. So very hot. All over.

She moistened dry lips. 'Jarrett—'

'Abbie...!' His lips moved against her temple now, gently caressing, his own breathing shallow. 'God, Abbie!' he groaned unsteadily. 'You're more intoxicating than any wine!'

This—being in Jarrett's arms—was more intoxicating than wine! Or perhaps it was the wine making her tingle all over in this way. She didn't know; what she did know was that she never wanted this to end.

She relaxed against him, her body curving more intimately into his, feeling the hard contours of his body,

the male strength of him, her arms entwining about the
back of his neck as his arms moved possessively about
her waist, any pretence they had previously given of
dancing formally together completely obliterated.

'I've wanted you since the moment I first looked at
you,' Jarrett groaned against her earlobe, nibbling gently
on the tender skin there.

Abbie felt a quiver of delight down her spine. '"The
man-hunter" or the "paper-bag job"?' she reminded
him satirically.

Jarrett moved back slightly to look down at her, winc-
ing as he saw the laughter glowing in her eyes. 'You
heard that?' he groaned.

'I certainly did,' she confirmed with a wide smile.

'You thought I was an arrogant fool before we were
even introduced!' he realised.

'I thought you were a misogynist,' she corrected him.

'It was only when you got to know me a little better
you thought I was an arrogant fool!'

'Never a fool, Jarrett.' She shook her head. 'A cynic,
perhaps, but not a fool.' And she wasn't far from being
a cynic herself; as Alison had pointed out at the time,
they were two of a kind. She viewed men as warily as
Jarrett viewed woman.

'All that talk about strawberry trifles and chocolate
éclairs!' he groaned self-disgustedly.

Abbie laughed. 'Out of interest, what was your final
verdict?'

'After that initial meeting?' He delayed, obviously not
happy with the question.

Abbie put her head back, looking up at him questioningly. 'Yes...'

He grimaced. 'You aren't going to like it.'

She shrugged. 'I learnt long ago to deal with things I don't like,' she assured him enigmatically.

Despite her efforts to make light of her statement, she could still sense Jarrett looking at her questioningly, only to be met with bland indifference as she returned his gaze. That was how she dealt with things she didn't like!

'Ice cream,' he told her bluntly. 'Delicious to look at, but cold to eat.'

She schooled herself to remain unmoved by the description, although inwardly she had to admit she felt hurt. He was wrong about her, so very wrong... 'And the next day?' she persisted. 'What did you think of me then?'

He sighed. 'Abbie—'

'Jarrett!' she prompted.

They were still dancing, moving slowly to the music, totally unaware of the other people dancing near them. In fact, totally unaware of anyone else in the room, their attention focused only on each other.

'Don't tell me,' Abbie decided. 'I just know I'm going to like this even less!'

Jarrett grimaced again. 'Still ice cream,' he admitted reluctantly.

It hurt. She would be lying if she said anything else, but by the same token she knew it was the impression she had aimed for for so many years. Ice cream. Cold. Emotionally removed.

'And now?' she pressed huskily.

'Ah, now.' Jarrett looked much more comfortable with 'now'. 'Baked Alaska in reverse,' he told her without hesitation.

'I beg your pardon?' Abbie looked up at him incredulously, totally baffled by the description.

'Have you ever eaten baked Alaska?'

'Yes...'

He nodded. 'Then you'll know it's ice cream in the middle and sweet meringue on the outside?'

Her eyes widened. 'And you think that I—'

'Cold ice is the façade you present to the world,' he confirmed. 'And sweet meringue is what you are inside.'

To say she was stunned would be an understatement; Jarrett was obviously coming to know her much better than she would wish!

It hadn't been too difficult keeping men at a distance these last few years, the majority accepting that cool façade she chose to present to the world. Those who were only interested in the Sutherland millions were easily dispatched.

Jarrett didn't belong to the latter category; he was as rich if not richer than she was, and he didn't accept her cold exterior as the real Abbie either...

'I want to get out of here, Abbie,' he told her gruffly. 'Take you back to my apartment, melt the ice cream and drown in the sweet meringue!' His eyes blazed deeply gold.

She swallowed hard, images of the two of them together flashing inside her head in spite of herself. Despite his opinion of women, she didn't doubt that Jarrett would be a considerate lover, unselfish, wanting his partner to know full pleasure before he allowed his own feelings to spiral out of control. The evocative images his words had given her made her tremble with anticipation of that pleasure.

She moistened her lips. 'Too much of a sweet thing can make you sick,' she warned huskily.

He shook his head. 'Maybe I'll be like Stephen and find I like baked Alaska best.' He throatily reminded her of that conversation in Canada.

Again she swallowed hard. 'Think of the tedium, Jarrett.' She reminded him of the same conversation.

He shrugged. 'Baked Alaska is one of those rare and unusual desserts.'

'But as a staple diet it could become nauseating,' Abbie persisted, feeling they were on very dangerous ground. In fact, the most dangerous thing about this conversation was that she was fast being seduced by it!

Jarrett looked down at her, his eyes searching. 'The thing is, Abbie, you aren't always baked Alaska. You're never that éclair I first likened you to, insubstantial on familiarity, but sometimes you're marshmallow, at others you're a brandy snap—but the one thing that you never are is tedious!'

Abbie stared at him, no longer even able to speak. What was she going to do?

'Come on.' He took a firm hold of her arm, turning her back towards their table as he made the decision for her. 'I'll pay the bill and we'll get out of here!'

She felt as if she was on a rollercoaster ride, with Jarrett at the helm. And she wasn't sure she wanted to get off!

She accompanied Jarrett as if in a daze, just the touch of his hand on her arm making her fully aware of him. This had never happened to her before, and it was with a man who angered her one moment and made her laugh the next! What—?

'Jarrett? Jarrett, it is you!' greeted a female voice before they actually reached their table. 'You didn't stay in Canada very long,' the woman added with haughty amusement, reaching up to kiss him warmly on the lips, her heady perfume easily discernible. 'Let me guess, the Black Widow eluded you yet again!' she taunted happily.

Abbie had felt the equivalent of an electric shock shoot through her at the first sound of that voice, but as the words the woman was saying penetrated that shock she felt a numbness starting to creep over her.

For the woman was none other than her own stepdaughter, Cathy Sutherland.

And, from the familiarity with which she had greeted Jarrett, the way she was talking, the two of them knew each other very well!

CHAPTER TEN

HIS worst nightmare had become reality!

What were the chances, the odds, of him meeting Cathy Sutherland, while in Abbie's company, before he had a chance to tell Abbie of his acquaintance with the other woman? Almost nil, he would have thought!

Yet it had happened. He could see by the rising coldness and disgust on Abbie's face that his oversight in not having been completely honest with her over Cathy before this was going to cost him dearly. And he didn't mean on a business level!

And Cathy's remark about the Black Widow—! Hell!

'I did try to tell you, Jarrett,' Cathy continued to make the situation worse. 'It's virtually impossible to—Sabina...!' She at last seemed to realise who Jarrett's companion was, openly staring at Abbie now, two bright spots of red becoming visible on her cheeks as her face slowly paled. She turned, incredulous, to Jarrett, before coming back to Abbie. 'My God, Jarrett,' she breathed. 'You did it. You actually got through the security system to the woman herself!' She gave that trilling laugh that had so grated on Jarrett's nerves on the other occasions he had met her, and did so even more now. 'You're looking very—glamorous, Sabina,' she drawled. 'It must be Jarrett's influence,' she added bitchily.

There really was no love lost between these two women; Jarrett could see that all too clearly as Abbie met the other woman's words with cold disdain. But, having heard how Cathy and her brother had tried to take Charlie away from her own mother purely for financial reasons, he certainly couldn't blame Abbie for her contempt of the older woman!

But as that violet gaze was turned on him he could see he was included in those feelings of contempt. Once again, he couldn't blame Abbie for feeling that way; she knew now he hadn't been completely honest with her. In fact, from the dislike he could feel emanating from her in his direction, he could tell that Abbie believed he had blatantly lied to her. It wasn't true, of course, but she didn't exactly look in the mood to listen to his explanation of having been economical with the truth!

Damn, damn, damn!

'Well, it looks as if I've interrupted your evening for long enough,' Cathy dismissed lightly. 'Do call me, Jarrett.' She reached out and touched the hardness of his cheek in a gesture that smacked of intimacy. 'I'm simply longing to hear all your news,' she trilled, before turning to Abbie, blue eyes glittering hardly, her mouth twisted into a scornful smile. 'Lovely to see you again, Sabina,' she added insincerely. 'Say hello to the brat for me.' She turned and walked away to rejoin her friends at a table across the room.

Jarrett had always wondered what a pregnant silence was like—now he knew! Cathy had walked away and left a tense silence behind her, full of expectation. Jarrett had a distinct feeling that blood might actually flow—his!

'Abbie—'

'I'm leaving, Jarrett,' she told him stonily. 'If you have any sense, you won't come with me.'

No one had ever credited him with sense—plenty of other things, but not sense! 'I'm coming with you,' he told her grimly, wanting to reach out and clasp her arm, but knowing it was the worst thing he could do at this particular moment. Completely unlike the woman who had flowed so easily in his arms on the dance floor, Abbie was now as tense as a taut piece of string, and if he attempted to touch her she was likely to snap, hitting out at the first available target—again him! 'We need to talk,' he insisted heavily.

'Talk!' She almost spat the word at him, eyes flashing deeply violet. 'I suggest you try talking to Cathy—she actually wants to talk to you!'

He gave a deep sigh. 'If you'll let me, Abbie, I can explain about Cathy—'

'I don't want your explanations, Jarrett, about anything.' She turned on him harshly, snatching up her bag from the table. 'You've already told me one lie that I know of—thanks to Cathy!—and anything else you have to say is, in my opinion, suspect!'

His mouth tightened at the insult. 'Your opinion would be wrong!' he bit out hardly.

Abbie gave him a look of withering disgust as she shook her head. 'I don't think so.'

'You aren't thinking at all at this moment,' he rasped, reaching out instinctively to touch her, realising too late it was the worst thing he could have done, Abbie flinching back as if he had just struck her. Minutes ago she had been fluid and warm in his arms; he had a sinking feeling that would never happen again. It would be pure luck on his part if Abbie ever allowed him near her again, and, the way his luck was going at the moment, he didn't stand a chance! 'Abbie, let's get out of here and talk. I'll explain about Cathy—'

'No—I'll explain about Cathy!' she told him vehemently, breathing hard, angry colour in her cheeks as she turned and strode forcefully out of the restaurant,

completely unaware of the male attention she received
as she did so.

But Jarrett was very aware of it, scowling at each and
every man who had watched Abbie's exit with interest,
totally ignoring the friendly wave Cathy Sutherland gave
him as they passed close by the table she sat at with her
group of friends. If it weren't for Cathy and her
damned—

No, he realised as he looked regretfully at the rigid-
ness of Abbie's shoulders as she walked ahead of him,
what had just happened, in view of his evasion where
Cathy was concerned, had been inevitable, if not now,
then at some time in the future. But even if he had told
Abbie the truth earlier he knew her reaction would have
been exactly the same. His acquaintance with Cathy, no
matter how fleeting or uninvolved on his part, would
always have received this censure from Abbie. An accident waiting to happen… And how it had happened!

Abbie waited impatiently for him in the foyer of the
restaurant as he paid the bill, totally dismissing the *maî-
tre d*'s worry that their hurried departure had anything
to do with the food or service. Obviously not too many
people left shortly after ten o'clock!

Abbie was stony-faced as she sat beside him in the
car, so controlled she looked as if she might break in
two. There was more than fast thinking and explanations
required here, Jarrett acknowledged inwardly, for the
first time in his life wishing he had even half of
Jonathan's charm or Jordan's cheeky humour. Neither of
those two would have had any trouble talking themselves out of this one, had got themselves out of more
scrapes with women than he wanted to even think about,
whereas he— He didn't usually bother, he realised
slowly; no woman had ever been important enough to

him for him ever to feel the need to justify, or explain, his actions to them...

What was so different about Abbie? Oh, he had been attracted to her from the first, had told her as much earlier this evening. And on better acquaintance he had come to know the strength, and vulnerability, of her, the gentleness in her when she was with her daughter, her mischievous sense of humour when dealing with his brothers. She was a complex and intriguing woman, the sort of woman it might be impossible ever to know completely, even after a lifetime spent together.

Which brought him back to her marriage to Daniel Sutherland. Had she loved her husband? Were they happy together? Why did she hold herself so aloof from the world?

But Jarrett knew, even if he got the answers to those questions, that there would be a hundred more he would want answered...

Abbie Sutherland fascinated him. She was—

'Where are we going?'

He snapped back into an awareness of their surroundings, rather than concentrating on the woman herself, realising as he did so that he had instinctively driven the car in the direction of his apartment.

Which was odd in itself. He always made it a rule never to take a woman home, had always found it more convenient to spend the night at the home of the woman he was currently involved with, and that way he could choose when he wanted to go. But he wasn't currently involved with Abbie, and so the same rule didn't apply...

'To my apartment,' he replied firmly. 'It will be more private for the sort of conversation I believe we're going to have,' he explained as she looked at him sharply.

'Any raised voices in your house and your friend Tony would come running!'

'Tony isn't my friend, he's my employee,' Abbie told him stiffly. 'And I never raise my voice.'

No, she didn't, he realised thoughtfully. She had been annoyed with him several times during their acquaintance, but she had always let him know in other ways how she felt rather than screaming and shouting at him. Although screaming and shouting might have been preferable now to this coldness.

'But I might,' he told her honestly.

Abbie shook her head. 'In that case you may as well take me straight to my home, and forget about the two of us talking; I don't like being shouted at, either!'

There were a hell of a lot of things this woman didn't like: shouting, being manhandled, him…! 'In that case,' he ground out tautly, 'I'll try my best not to shout.'

'I would advise you to do more than try,' she told him scathingly. 'At the first sound of a raised voice, I'll leave.'

'Okay,' he agreed impatiently, hands tightly gripping the steering-wheel. 'I won't shout. God, you want your pound of flesh, don't you?' He might be fascinated by this woman, but he wasn't about to grovel!

'Only a pound, Jarrett?' she returned sarcastically. 'Believe me, that isn't nearly enough!'

He was glad to see that she seemed to be recovering some of her sense of humour, but was not so pleased that it seemed to be at his expense. Women; he would never understand them! And this woman least of all…

His apartment was serviceable rather than homely, he realised as he tried to see its expensive elegance through Abbie's no doubt critical eyes—they were sure to be critical; she had no reason to think of him any other way at the moment. It was a well-furnished apartment, open-plan lounge and dining area, gadget-orientated kitchen—anything to make life easier for him had to be worth it, and he couldn't always eat out!—with two bedrooms, both *en suite*. Although, of course, Abbie couldn't see the kitchen or the bedrooms. It was probably as well she couldn't see the latter; after he had left her this morning he had tried to get rid of some of his jet lag by going to bed for a couple of hours, and as far as he could remember he hadn't remade the bed, and his cleaner hadn't been in.

'Drink?' He indicated the selection of bottles on the side-dresser.

Abbie stood unyielding across the room from him. 'Will I need one?' she returned spikily.

'I do,' he acknowledged with a grimace. 'So you may as well join me.'

'In that case, a liqueur,' she accepted. 'Tia Maria, if you have it, please.'

He did, and he was glad of the few minutes' respite from the tension between them as he poured their drinks. Now that he had Abbie here, he wasn't sure what to say to her...! And feelings of uncertainty weren't emotions he was comfortable with.

He handed Abbie her drink before sipping his own whisky, grateful for its stinging warmth. He had a feeling that the next few minutes were going to be critical to any future relationship he might have with Abbie—if there was to be a future relationship!

He swallowed down another gulp of the fiery alcohol before speaking. 'I met Cathy several months ago.' He came straight to the point—as was his way. 'I admit, I struck up the acquaintance for reasons of my own, but—'

'She was your "reliable source",' Abbie guessed.

'Up to a point,' he allowed guardedly.

Abbie gave him a scathing sweep with those deep violet-coloured eyes. 'And which point would that be?' she asked sceptically.

'The point where she had the information I wanted,' he answered tautly.

'Concerning me?' Abbie prompted quietly.

'Yes,' he replied abruptly. This evening hadn't gone at all as he had planned, and neither had this conversation; he was on the defensive, and he didn't damn well like the feeling!

'And exactly what form, may I ask, did this "acquaintance" take?'

'I haven't slept with her, if that's what you're asking!' His eyes blazed deeply golden. 'Credit me with some taste, if you please, Abbie.'

She gave an unconcerned gesture. 'Most men seem to find Cathy more than attractive.'

'Then most men must be blind, or just stupid!' he said harshly. 'Cathy Sutherland has more notches on her bedpost than I care to think about—and I certainly don't intend being one of them!'

Abbie smiled without humour. 'I hear it's a rather magnificent four-poster.'

'I wouldn't know,' he returned savagely.

'No,' Abbie sighed, some of her tension seeming to leave her, 'I can see that you don't.' She sank down gracefully into one of the armchairs, suddenly looking small and vulnerable in its padded plushness. 'And it must be easy to see that there is no love lost between Daniel's eldest daughter and myself,' she added evenly.

He nodded. 'And I understand exactly why you feel the way you do.'

Abbie became very still, her eyes suddenly huge in the paleness of her face. 'How do you—? I can believe a lot of things of Cathy,' she confessed. 'But not that. I can't believe she told you how she tried to take Charlie away from me.' She shook her head. 'Cathy—'

'Didn't tell me,' Jarrett cut in softly, seeing the pained memories of that time in the darkness of Abbie's eyes.

She looked at him searchingly. 'Another reliable source, Jarrett?' she finally said slowly, once again on her guard.

'Loyal and loving friends doing everything they could to protect you—especially from me!' he explained ruefully.

She frowned at him, her frown turning to dismay as she realised exactly which friends he was referring to. 'I see,' she said, her expression pained.

'I can see that you don't,' he denied impatiently, moving down on his haunches beside the chair she sat in. 'Abbie, Alison and Stephen—'

'Let me down,' she finished dazedly. 'I never thought Alison would— We've been friends for such a long time—good friends, I thought—'

'They're both still your friend, Abbie,' Jarrett insisted forcefully. 'They only wanted me to understand why you keep people at a distance, why you employ people like Tony—' He broke off as she suddenly pushed past him to stand up. 'Abbie...?'

'I have to go,' she muttered, looking about her distractedly for somewhere to put her glass down.

'Abbie—'

'I have to go!' she repeated in an anguished voice. 'I have to go,' she said dully.

'Not like this.' Jarrett straightened, taking the glass

out of her trembling fingers and putting it down beside his own on the coffee-table.

'How else do you want me to go?' she choked emotionally, tears swimming in her eyes as she looked up at him. 'What else is it you want to know, Jarrett? What else did Alison and Stephen tell you?' she went on brokenly. 'Did they tell you about my marriage to Daniel, too? Did they tell you that I hated being married to him? That for five years I endured being his wife, his sexual plaything? Did they—?'

'Don't do this to yourself, Abbie,' Jarrett groaned protestingly, grasping the tops of her arms.

These were questions he had wanted answers to, but not at this price, never at the pain it was causing Abbie to recall it. And that pain was immense. Gone was that coldly aloof woman, and in her place was a trembling child, a child who, unlike Charlie, had no one to protect her.

He wanted to protect her, to take away all that hurt and suffering, but at the same time he knew he was helping cause it. Abbie obviously managed to survive, emotionally, by burying all of this somewhere deep inside her where it could never be touched, need never be looked at. But he had unwittingly made her do both those things. The result stripped her of all defences.

'Don't, Abbie,' he groaned again, gathering her close into his arms, holding her there, wanting to keep her there until he had wiped away all the pain. 'I don't want to know, don't need to know!' And he didn't.

This woman was unlike anyone he had ever met before. Or was ever likely to meet again. And he didn't want anyone ever to be able to hurt her again. Including himself.

His hands moved so that he cradled each side of her

beautiful face, a face wet with tears, tears he had caused to fall. He gently kissed those tears away, tasting their salt, feeling the way Abbie trembled against him, sensing that she was pulling away from him, that he had crossed over another line of defence. And he didn't want her to have defences against him!

'I won't hurt you, Abbie,' he assured her tenderly. 'I don't ever want to hurt you.'

Pained violet-blue eyes looked up into his. 'Then leave me alone, Jarrett,' she pleaded. 'Stay away from me!'

'Let you go back into your ivory tower?' He shook his head in answer to his own question. 'You don't belong there, Abbie. You're warm, and caring, a beautiful woman—'

'I'm just another notch you want to add to your bedpost,' she returned cynically. 'I was a virgin when I married Daniel, Jarrett. There has been no one in my life since he died. And my bedposts are brass. They have no notches on!'

He had already guessed that she hadn't been involved with anyone after her marriage, but it came as something of a surprise to him that she had been untouched when she married. The physical side of her marriage to Daniel Sutherland had not been a happy one from what she had said...

'It doesn't always have to be like your marriage, Abbie,' he told her gently. 'Lovemaking should be something beautiful, shared between two people who care about each other, who want to give and receive pleasure.'

She met his gaze unflinchingly. 'Has it ever been like that for you, Jarrett?' she said pointedly.

He felt as if she had reached out and slapped him. Sex

was something he enjoyed, and obviously it was more enjoyable for him if his bed partner found pleasure too. But he knew that wasn't what Abbie was asking him...

'I can tell by your expression that it hasn't,' she continued, moving away from him. 'The cynic preaching to the unconvincible. I'm sure you're right, Jarrett, otherwise there would be no relationships, and certainly no marriages. But for some people it can't be that way—'

'Not you, Abbie,' he cut in firmly. 'I don't believe it.'

'Why?' She raised dark brows, back under control again now. 'Because of the way I look?' She dismissed her model figure and classically beautiful features. 'That's no proof of anything, Jarrett,' she added sadly.

'But if you never give it a chance—'

'I gave it a chance!' she put in vehemently. 'Do you think I wanted my marriage to be like that?' Her eyes sparkled with anger now rather than tears. 'Of course I didn't,' she snapped. 'It just happened.'

Jarrett's mouth tightened. 'If Daniel Sutherland was anywhere near as self-interested as his children, then I'm not surprised!'

Her head rose, her expression becoming blank. 'I don't want to talk about Daniel. Or his children. In fact—' she turned to pick up her bag '—I don't believe we have anything more to say to each other.'

She was leaving. Obviously with the intention of never seeing him again.

He didn't want that to happen. He had to see her again!

Why?

He instantly recoiled from answering that, even to himself. And he had never had any difficulty in being honest with himself...

Why had he chased after her from Canada? Why had

it been so important that he see her again? And why, tonight, when Cathy had revealed their acquaintance to Abbie, had he been so desperate that she wouldn't walk out on him?

The answers to those questions were inside him somewhere, and until he had them perhaps it would be better if he and Abbie didn't see each other...

'Perhaps not personally,' he accepted harshly. 'But my business offer still stands,' he added, eyes narrowed.

Abbie looked bored by the subject. 'I've already told you to send over your proposals, Jarrett,' she advised him uninterestedly.

His mouth twisted. 'Will you read them?'

'Of course I'll read them,' she clipped. 'I never allow my personal feelings to interfere with business.'

If the feelings she had revealed towards her husband were anything to go by, then that was definitely true! Why had she married the man, feeling about him as she did? Could Cathy possibly be right in her claim? Had Abbie married Daniel Sutherland for his money?

'But perhaps it would be better, for all concerned, if in future I dealt with Jonathan or Jordan,' Abbie suggested tersely.

Again he felt that burning rage at the thought of either of his brothers being anywhere near Abbie. They were more than capable of negotiating a deal with Abbie—it was what else they might negotiate that bothered him! Jonathan was smooth and charming, a combination Jarrett had never known to fail his brother where women were concerned, and Jordan had had no difficulty in making Abbie laugh from the beginning. But if one of them succeeded with her where he had failed—!

'Fine,' he barked. 'Would you like me to drive you home?'

'That won't be necessary.' She gave a small smile. 'Tim will be waiting downstairs with the car.'

Tony was allowed to stay home, but obviously Tim wasn't! Had the other man been following them all evening? Probably—and Jarrett hadn't even noticed! This woman was surrounded like a fortress!

'You had better not keep him waiting any longer, then, had you?' Jarrett returned tightly.

'No,' she agreed. 'Thank you for dinner, Jarrett. It was—informative,' she added in parting.

Jarrett watched her go, his apartment, his own personal space, suddenly seeming very empty without Abbie in it. Damn it, what was wrong with him? He felt angry and agitated—very agitated. He had wanted Abbie tonight, he accepted that—damn it, he had wanted her that first night too. But she was just a woman, like any other woman.

But she wasn't, that betraying voice inside his head whispered.

Yes, she was, damn it! She was also a woman who had married a man thirty years older than she was, a man she'd admitted she had hated being married to. Much as he shied away from the idea, didn't want to believe such a thing of Abbie, maybe she was mercenary, after all...

She was definitely a lot more complicated than most women, which just made her more trouble. He was well out of that relationship.

Well out of it...

CHAPTER ELEVEN

'MR HUNTER to see you, Mrs Sutherland.' The young maid stood expectantly at the door after making her announcement.

Abbie looked up from the game of snakes and ladders she was playing with Charlie, her heart beating erratically at the name Hunter. 'Which Mr Hunter, Mary?' she prompted guardedly.

'Jarrett!' Charlie jumped up excitedly, the game forgotten. 'It has to be Jarrett.'

It didn't have to be anything of the kind. In fact, Abbie sincerely hoped it wasn't! The last week had been relatively peaceful—Jarrett-free! And it had taken that long for Abbie to recover her equilibrium from that evening she had spent with him. It had been a mistake, in more ways than one!

Firstly, she had learnt of Jarrett's friendship with Cathy, a woman who was her arch-enemy, the older woman having disliked Abbie intensely from the day her father had taken Abbie home and announced his intention of marrying her. That Jarrett had been made aware of the two women's dislike of each other, and behaved accordingly, did not excuse the fact that he had evaded admitting knowing Cathy when Abbie had asked him earlier.

Secondly, she had blurted out how she felt about Daniel, about being married to him. And that was something she had never done before, with anyone. Oh, friends like Alison and Stephen had guessed that she wasn't happy, but they had never probed into her reasons for marrying a man she didn't love, or why she had stayed married to him when it was so obvious she wasn't happy with him. Yet after knowing Jarrett only a few days she had told him all of that. Except why she had married Daniel at all... At least that was something!

But thirdly, and more seriously, Jarrett had managed to breach the barrier that kept Abbie removed from those around her. She wasn't even sure how that had happened, but, no matter how she tried to deny it to herself, she knew that until Cathy had interrupted them she had been quite willing to go along with Jarrett and let him melt the ice cream!

Of the three, that was the one she had the most problem accepting. What was it about Jarrett that had made her willing—eager, even!—to break all the rules she had made for herself the last few years? That was an answer she dared not find!

This last week, with no contact from him, she had managed to persuade herself—almost!—that that weakness had never happened...

And now he was here—again! Her heart was beating too fast, her cheeks felt hot and flushed, and there was a slight tremble to her hands as she raised them to straighten her hair into its confining plait down her spine.

'I'm afraid I don't know.' Mary looked confused by the question. 'He just said his name was Hunter...'

Which could mean Jonathan, Jordan—or Jarrett.

Mary looked worried at her hesitation. 'Shall I go back and ask?'

'No, that's fine, Mary,' Abbie dismissed briskly, realising she was behaving like a gauche schoolgirl. 'Ask him to come in.' And take your time about it, she inwardly added.

Charlie was leaping up and down in excitement at the thought of seeing Jarrett again, the game of snakes and ladders completely abandoned, and Abbie took those few moments' respite to compose herself before Mr Hunter entered the room.

Her relief was immense seconds later when it was Jonathan who breezed cheerfully in. Charlie, who had been in the process of launching herself on Jarrett, instantly faltered, totally confused as she stared at the tall blond-haired man with warm golden eyes.

Jonathan smiled at the little girl. 'You must be Charlie,' he said in a friendly tone. 'Jarrett's told me all about you.'

Charlie blinked, not at all sure of this tall stranger with the smile. 'He has?' she said uncertainly.

Jonathan nodded. 'You ski very well—and you're as beautiful as your mother!' he added knowingly.

Charlie gave a shy grin. 'Did Jarrett really say that about me?'

'He certainly did,' Jonathan nodded. 'I'm Jarrett's younger brother, Jonathan.'

Charlie's eyes were wide with surprise. 'You don't look like him,' she said suspiciously.

Jonathan looked unabashed. 'I'm the good-looking one!'

'And the charmer,' Abbie put in, fully recovered now from the fact that Mr Hunter wasn't Jarrett, after all. A part of her, although she was still loath to admit it, was disappointed that it wasn't him...

What was happening to her?

'You're only saying that because it's true,' Jonathan drawled lazily. 'Poor Jarrett hasn't got a clue!'

'There's nothing "poor" about Jarrett,' Abbie returned swiftly.

He raised his blond brows. 'Have you seen my big brother recently?' he asked, his attention suddenly caught by the game on the coffee-table they had been playing before his arrival. 'Snakes and ladders...' He walked over to look more closely at the board. 'Who has the blue marker?' He referred to the player who was obviously well in the lead of the red marker.

'Me.' Charlie joined him beside the table. 'Mummy has just gone down the long snake there.' She pointed to the board, her shyness rapidly evaporating.

Jonathan went down on his haunches beside the little girl. 'That's the trouble with snakes, Charlie,' he murmured. 'They sneak up on you when you're least expecting them!' He glanced up pointedly at Abbie as he spoke this last remark.

'Actually,' Abbie put in, his double meaning not lost on her, 'I crept up on this particular snake.'

'I believe you did,' he acknowledged. He straightened, his expression confrontational as he met Abbie's gaze.

She continued to look at him for several long seconds, but she was finally the one to turn away. 'Charlie, could you go and ask Mary to bring in tea for all of us? I take it you do drink tea?' She turned enquiringly back to Jonathan.

He grimaced. 'It has been known—with aged aunts, and an alcohol-disapproving father!'

Abbie had completely forgotten about this man's mother, and the problem she seemed to have with men! 'I think, as it's only four o'clock, we may as well stick to the tea—irrespective of aged aunts and fathers!' she pronounced.

'Perhaps there's some cherry cake, too!' Charlie said expectantly as she skipped from the room.

Jonathan watched her departure. 'Nice child,' he murmured appreciatively. 'She's a credit to you, Abbie.'

'Thank you,' she accepted awkwardly, still uncertain
as to the reason he was here at all.

She had received Jarrett's offer for Sutherland Hotels
several days ago, and in view of the problems there were
with the hotels the offer was certainly a reasonable one.
Copies of those proposals had been duly forwarded to
Cathy and Danny—and as quickly returned with an
agreement to the offer. As Abbie had expected they
would. But she was still looking at the offer herself, and
she wasn't about to be hurried over it, by any of the
Hunter family!

'This is—unexpected, Jonathan,' she told him.

'Mind if I sit down?' It was a perfunctory request,
because even as he asked the question he was in the act
of sitting down in one of the armchairs, that warm,
charming smile curving his lips.

Abbie gave a rueful smile in return. 'Does that usually
get you where you want to go?' she teased. 'The smile,'
she explained at his puzzled expression.

That smile became a wide grin. 'Usually,' he replied.

Abbie frowned. 'And why do you want to be here?'
she said.

'I'm on an errand of mercy,' he told her. 'Strictly on
a personal level, of course.'

'Of course,' she acknowledged. 'Although I have no
idea what you're talking about!'

He sighed. 'I'm talking about working with a man
who snarls and growls at you, when he speaks at all, a
man who believes that the twenty-four hours in each day
should all be spent working, that things like eating and
sleeping are unnecessary luxuries and not to be bothered
with!' he concluded wearily.

Jarrett... He had to be talking about Jarrett!

She moistened dry lips. 'What does all of that have to do with me?'

'Are you kidding?' Jonathan groaned. 'Everything! I would say it has everything to do with you.' He looked across at her with golden eyes. Eyes so like Jarrett's... 'Abbie, why are you giving him such a hard time?'

Jarrett was having a hard time! He wasn't the only one who had become a workaholic this last week. Nor was he the only one that couldn't sleep at night. Which was the very reason she was working so hard; it was impossible to sleep when all her thoughts kept returning again and again to the night she had dinner with Jarrett, and the only way to block out those thoughts was to fill her hours with work!

'I believe you're mistaken, Jonathan, in coming to your conclusion about the reason for Jarrett's excessive behaviour,' she told him coolly. 'He sounds as if he is behaving perfectly normally—for him!—to me.'

Jonathan gave her a searching look, a look Abbie had trouble withstanding, finally able to turn away as Charlie came back into the room accompanied by Mary carrying the laden tea-tray.

'Cook says she is just about to bake some cakes,' Charlie informed Abbie, eyes bright. 'She says I can help her.'

And leave Abbie alone once again with Jonathan— who was proving as much of an intrusion to her privacy as Jarrett! But Charlie loved baking cakes, and it would be unfair of her to say no. 'Just don't eat too many of them and then not be able to manage your dinner,' she warned her daughter lightly as Charlie left with Mary.

'How long have you been widowed, Abbie?'

She frowned sharply across at Jonathan, disconcerted

by the directness of his question. But then, what could she expect from the brother of Jarrett?

'I don't think that is any of your business, Jonathan.' She prickled, moving forward to pour the tea for them both.

'Not long enough, by the look of you,' he drawled, leaning forward to take the cup she held out to him. 'That stepdaughter of yours is one hell of a bitch, isn't she?' he said.

Abbie stiffened. 'You've met Cathy too?'

'Briefly. Very briefly,' he repeated. 'She came to the office to see Jarrett a couple of days ago. He wouldn't even let her in the door, told her exactly what he thought of her in about a dozen succinct words, warned her to stay well away from both you and Charlie in future, and told her to get out. Which, after a few well-chosen words of her own—' he grimaced at the memory '—she promptly did!'

Abbie was shaken by the fact that Jarrett had seen Cathy again, although, from the sound of it, it hadn't been a very pleasant meeting! Jarrett had warned Cathy to stay away from her. That sounded decidedly protective to her. Or, worse, possessive…!

'And Cathy's "well-chosen words" were…?' she prompted Jonathan softly.

For once he looked disconcerted, avoiding her probing gaze. 'As I've already said, she's one hell of a bitch!' he finally muttered.

Abbie sat down. 'Those words were about me,' she guessed easily.

Jonathan looked uncomfortable. 'I never said that.'

'You didn't need to.' Abbie shook her head. 'It's okay, Jonathan, Cathy's never made any secret of the fact that she hates me.'

When Abbie was first married to Daniel, she had found Cathy's resentful behaviour towards her hurtful, especially as she was trying to come to terms with being married at all, and to a man who didn't even pretend to love her! She had been another Sutherland possession, like the Sutherland plane, the Rolls-Royce, the large houses, the Rolex on Daniel's wrist—all beautiful accessories to show off his wealth and power. Daniel had had a weakness for beautiful possessions, and Sabina, as a much sought-after model, beautiful, and thirty years younger than him, had been the diamond in the king's crown!

Jonathan pulled another face. 'As I said, one hell of a—'

'Jonathan,' Abbie cut in firmly, knowing he was playing for time. She couldn't exactly blame him; Cathy had a habit, when it came to Abbie, of forgetting she was a wealthy lady, and began acting like a fishwife!

He let out a deep breath. 'She said something along the lines that the only things you have going for you are a beautiful face and a whore's body—and that you ensnared her father with both of them!'

Abbie wasn't in the least shocked, had heard it all before, often put more graphically, if anything.

'And that you had obviously now done the same thing with Jarrett,' Jonathan added quietly.

That didn't upset Abbie either; in fact, she laughed! The thought of her behaving in that way with any man was highly unlikely, but the idea that Jarrett, with his inborn cynicism, would be taken in by it was even more ridiculous. Jarrett, who prided himself on having no weaknesses, and, where women were concerned, having no illusions whatsoever—absurd!

'I remember you when you were modelling, you

know, Abbie,' Jonathan told her warmly. 'You used to be in magazines and the newspapers all the time. And then suddenly you disappeared. I could hardly believe my luck last week when we came to your office with Jarrett; there you were, and as gorgeous as ever!'

'How touching!' rasped a scornful voice.

They both turned towards the sound of that voice—Jarrett's voice—a flustered-looking Mary standing just in front of him in the doorway. Jarrett, with his usual arrogance, hadn't waited to be announced, but had followed the maid to the sitting-room. He obviously hadn't liked the brief part of the conversation he had overheard between Abbie and Jonathan!

'Mr Hunter,' Mary announced with another worried look in Abbie's direction. Just how many of them were there? her bemused expression seemed to say!

Too many, Abbie inwardly acknowledged. 'Thank you, Mary,' she dismissed pleasantly, waiting until the young girl had gone before turning back to Jarrett.

Jonathan was right—he did look grim. Jarrett's face was thinner, and consequently harder, and the dark hollows below his eyes indicated the lack of sleep Jonathan had also hinted at. But Abbie shied away from the explanation Jonathan had given for these changes in his older brother; Jarrett was a man whose heart was encased in ice where women were concerned!

'Jarrett,' she greeted coolly.

'Abbie,' he replied in a voice liberally laced with sarcasm.

'This is a surprise,' she returned evenly.

Dark brows rose over stony golden eyes. 'Did you say the same thing to Jonathan when he arrived?'

His meaning was quite clear, and Abbie felt the angry colour burning in her cheeks. Did he really think—?

After all she had told him about herself, about her marriage, did he really believe that she and Jonathan—?

'Actually, no.' Jonathan was the one to answer him in a clear voice as he slowly rose to his feet. 'But then, Charlie was so pleased to meet me, I don't think Abbie had time to be surprised. I thought you were in a meeting this afternoon?'

'And I thought, until I saw your car outside, you were going through the final draft of a contract,' Jarrett returned hardly.

'All done, and sitting on your desk awaiting your inspection,' Jonathan assured him lightly.

Jarrett's mouth twisted. 'And so you thought you would just pay Abbie a call?'

'Why not?' His brother sounded casual. 'You didn't mention you were coming here, either,' he reasoned.

Jarrett didn't look in the mood to be reasoned with! 'It appears my decision to visit was as spontaneous as yours!' he barked.

'Doesn't it?' Jonathan nodded happily, not at all bothered by his older brother's obvious aggression. In fact, he seemed to be enjoying it!

Like two little boys, Abbie decided, one of them angry because he thought the other one had usurped his toy. Only she wasn't a toy, and she belonged to neither of these two men!

'I am rather busy,' she told them both pointedly.

'Not too busy for tea, it seems,' Jarrett rasped as he looked at their used cups.

'The chink's getting bigger, Jarrett,' Jonathan warned softly. 'Careful now, or else some of the flesh and blood may begin to show, and then we'll all know you're human, after all!'

It was as well there was obviously a strong bond of

brotherly love between these two men, otherwise Jonathan would never have dared to talk to Jarrett in this way. Even so, it was obvious to Abbie that Jarrett was far from pleased at the taunt. As was borne out by his next comment!

'Oh, shut up, Jonathan!' His patience had completely gone now. 'If you have nothing of any relevance to say, I suggest you don't say anything at all!'

'Don't look so worried, Abbie,' Jonathan said breezily at her obvious concern. 'Jarrett's talked to Jordan and me like this since we were little kids.'

'And a lot of good it did me!' Jarrett scorned. 'Both of you still go your own sweet way—as evidenced by today. Just out of interest, Jonathan, what the hell are you doing here?' he demanded.

'The same as you, probably,' his brother returned unhelpfully.

Jarrett was not amused. 'And what, precisely, might that be?'

'Business, of course,' Jonathan announced airily. 'I called to see if Abbie was having any problems with the contract we sent to her last week. But now that the boss is here I'm quite happy to leave you to deal with any problems that Abbie might have!'

With that *double entendre* left hanging in the air, and a light kiss placed on one of Abbie's burning cheeks, he exited the room, and presumably the house!

CHAPTER TWELVE

DAMN Jonathan, Jarrett inwardly cursed, not for the first time regretting the easy familiarity with people that he had encouraged in both his brothers. Never be in fear, or awe, of anyone, he had taught them. Perhaps he should have made it clearer that didn't include him!

God, Abbie looked good, utterly beautiful in the deep blue cashmere sweater and a navy fitted skirt, her legs long and tanned. Only her hair was wrong; he much preferred it loose down her spine.

Left alone, the two of them simply stared at each other. Jarrett because he was hungry for the sight of her, Abbie because he could see she was still wary of him.

The last week had been hell as far as Jarrett was concerned, each successive twenty-four hours more difficult to get through than the last. And it wasn't that he hadn't tried to make it easy on himself, had invited out—on separate occasions, of course!—two of the women he had always, in the past, enjoyed spending time with.

Delia was hot chocolate cake, lush and seductive, usually delicious and Mandy was lemon sorbet, light and refreshing, equally delicious in her own way. Delia had been as warm and wonderful as ever, and Mandy as sharp and witty, but his heart hadn't been in either evening, and he had ended up going home alone shortly after midnight on both evenings, memories of baked Alaska preventing him from even escaping into the oblivion of sleep. He had found himself cursing the ex-

162

istence of the divine Abbie Sutherland on more than one occasion!

Finally, to the extent that he had decided, this morning, in fact, the only way to deal with this particular craving was to completely gorge himself on it until, as Abbie had said herself, he became nauseous. Which was what he was doing here now. Only to find his damned brother already here, and obviously chatting quite amiably with the woman he, Jarrett, wanted!

He looked across at her with deeply golden eyes. 'Do you have any problems, Abbie?' he asked, wishing she had felt half the hunger for him this last week that he had felt for her. And knowing that it wasn't so... Abbie didn't need anyone, least of all him!

'None that I can think of, Jarrett, no,' she returned. 'We did have a minor difficulty with one of the taps in the lower—'

'I meant with the contract,' he cut in gratingly; her mockery, feeling as raw as he did, was the last thing he wanted!

To his surprise, Abbie smiled. 'I'm well aware of what you meant, Jarrett. Can I get you some tea?' she offered politely.

Politeness; was that what their relationship had deteriorated to? Politeness was reserved for respect of the elderly, for complete strangers—or people you wanted to keep at a distance...? Why would Abbie want to keep him at a distance? Perhaps she wasn't quite as immune to the awareness between them as she pretended to be! What did he have to lose?

He met her gaze steadily for several moments, reassured slightly by the fact that she was the one to look away. 'I would rather we just went to bed,' he told her softly.

She looked stunned by the directness of his statement. And then her cheeks coloured fiery-red. 'I—'

'Don't say no straight away, Abbie.' He moved closer to her. 'There's something between the two of us. I don't know what it is—'

'An over-vivid imagination on your part, by the sound of it!' she scoffed, looking away.

'Don't turn away from me, Abbie,' he rasped, reaching out to grasp her arms, his restraint—what little he had left after a frustrating and sleepless week!—having vanished completely. 'I'm not in the mood for games!'

She looked up at him with defiant violet-blue eyes. 'What are you in the mood for, Jarrett?' she challenged. 'A few hours' romp in bed, and then move on to the next woman?' She shook her head. 'I've told you—ad nauseum!—that I don't have affairs.'

'This may not be just an affair,' he grated. 'But if we don't try, we'll never know,' he pleaded persuasively.

'Does that line usually work?' she taunted.

'This isn't a "line", damn it!' His voice rose angrily. 'I'm telling you how I feel. And—'

'And I'm telling you I don't want to know how you feel!' she returned cuttingly. But Jarrett was sure, when he looked into her eyes, that he could see tears glistening there... 'I like my life the way it is—'

'I don't believe you,' he said quietly, those tears giving him encouragement, hope.

'Jarrett—'

'I—don't—believe—you—Abbie,' he repeated firmly, his arms moving about the slenderness of her waist as he pulled her into the warmth of his body.

He needed this, had hungered for it, and he couldn't take no for an answer. Maybe Abbie would hate him for it. But maybe she wouldn't...

He kissed her. It was almost like going to heaven, to

feel her soft and pliant in his arms, to feel the response
of her mouth against his. And she was responding, he
realised with increasing exhilaration. If this was heaven,
then he just wanted to stay here, to lose himself in
Abbie's enveloping warmth. It was—

Abbie wrenched her mouth away from his, those tears
he had seen glistening in her eyes earlier now cascading
down her cheeks. 'I can't do this, Jarrett,' she choked,
her eyes bruised pools of deep purple.

He still held onto her, refused to let her go completely.
'You were doing just fine,' he assured her huskily.

She avoided his gaze, staring down at the carpet at
their feet. 'I'm not, Jarrett. I can't—I don't— There's
been no one in my life since Daniel!'

'You already told me that,' he said gently. But she
was only twenty-seven, for God's sake, couldn't mean
to spend the rest of her life alone like this.

She looked up at him with eyes so full of pain he
almost flinched at all that concentrated raw emotion. 'I
hated being married,' she said flatly.

His mouth twisted. 'We both know I'm not asking you
to marry me, Abbie.'

'We both know you're being deliberately obtuse!' She
wrenched away from him, putting several feet between
them.

'No, I'm not, Abbie,' he assured her. 'Hell, I'm not
completely insensitive, you know. I realise that when
you say you hated being married what you really mean
is that you hated going to bed with your husband!'

'Yes...!' She shuddered with revulsion, her arms
wrapped about herself, as if to ward off an unwanted
touch.

'That doesn't mean you'll hate making love with me,'
he persisted, keeping his distance, accepting that in her

present frame of mind she was likely to run if he made any overt moves towards her. And would keep on running...

She drew in a ragged breath. 'I don't want to find out!'

This went so much deeper than simply an unhappy marriage. A lot of people had those, if the statistics— and his own parents' marriage!—were anything to go by. But those people survived. His own father had suffered through almost twenty years of living with a wife who was consistently unfaithful to him, and yet he had remarried, was happy in that second marriage. No, it wasn't marriage Abbie had a problem with, it was the physical intimacy that went along with the relationship...

'Why did you marry him, Abbie?'

She gave him a startled look. 'What?'

Jarrett smiled at her reassuringly. 'Let's sit down— Please, Abbie,' he prompted quietly as she automatically went to refuse. 'I have no intention of leaving yet.' He sat down in one of the armchairs. 'So we may as well be comfortable.'

From her troubled expression she obviously wasn't happy with his delay in leaving, but she did sit down— noticeably in the armchair as far away from his as it could be! That didn't matter; at the moment it was more important that he talk to her. Which was something, he realised, he had never felt the need to do with a woman before!

'Why, Abbie?' he prompted after the silence had stretched between them for several long, tension-filled minutes.

She raised her head. 'Because he asked me to,' she bit out defiantly.

Jarrett smiled. 'I'm sure he was far from the first man to do that!'

She shrugged. 'But Daniel was rich and powerful. Very rich, in fact, and so much older than me.'

Jarrett had stiffened instinctively at her admission that she had married a man with money. But that last admission gave the previous one a hollowness that simply didn't ring true. 'He was still in his fifties when he died, Abbie,' he reminded her dryly, sure now she was deliberately trying to alienate him with her implication of being interested in Daniel Sutherland's money.

She shrugged, looking down at her linked hands. 'He was ill for some time before he died.'

'How long?'

'Jarrett—'

'How long, Abbie?' he repeated firmly. 'I'm sure you can remember; it isn't that long ago!'

There were angry spots of colour in her cheeks as she glared at him. 'I'm sure Cathy was only too willing to tell you what a gold-digger I am—'

'I'm not interested in Cathy Sutherland's opinion— about anything!' he said scornfully.

'But you and she are such good friends—'

'This isn't going to work, Abbie,' he cut in, not fooled for a minute by her effort to change the subject. 'You know damn well that Cathy and I aren't friends. I admit she was useful for a while, and I'm not particularly proud of my part in that deception, but the woman can go to hell as far as I'm concerned!'

Abbie's lips curved. 'I have no doubt that one day she will!'

'How long was your husband ill before he died, Abbie?' Jarrett persisted.

Her mouth set into a stubborn line. 'I don't see what that has to do with—'

'Abbie!'

Her eyes flashed deeply purple as she glared at him again. 'Don't shout at me!' she snapped angrily. 'I've already told you that I don't like to be shouted at.'

'Then—answer—the—damned—question,' he bit out in a controlled voice. She was right; she had warned him about shouting at her. If only she weren't so damned infuriating! Usually you couldn't stop a woman from talking; this one was like a clam!

'Daniel was ill for several months before he died,' she finally answered him.

'And you were married for how long? Five years.' He answered his own question. 'So he wasn't ill when you married him. On the surmise of three score years and ten, Daniel Sutherland had another seventeen years to live, at least, when you married him.' Jarrett looked across at her with assessing eyes. 'That doesn't exactly fit in with the picture you're trying to give me of your having married an old man so that when he died you would inherit his money! Besides,' he added softly, 'you didn't inherit it, did you? Did you love him when you married him?'

'Jarrett, will you just let this go—?'

'I can't, Abbie,' he told her bluntly. 'It's too important.'

She swallowed hard. 'No, I didn't love Daniel when I married him,' she admitted with a shuddering sigh.

'So, you didn't love him. You hated being married to him. And you didn't want his money.' They were all statements, which allowed Jarrett time to formulate his thoughts. Suddenly the answer came to him...! 'Who were you protecting, Abbie?' he guessed shrewdly. 'And why?'

The angry colour faded from her cheeks. In fact, all colour faded from her face, leaving her pale and hollow-eyed, suddenly very young and vulnerable, reminding Jarrett all too forcibly that she was ten years younger than him. And, like him, she had suffered a lot.

'Who, Abbie?' He pushed her again. 'And why?'

She stared at him. Just stared at him. Seeming transfixed by the question.

CHAPTER THIRTEEN

ABBIE couldn't move. She felt mesmerised, glued to her chair.

How could Jarrett—? How did he—? What—?

She cleared her swollen throat. 'This doesn't have anything to do with you, Jarrett,' she finally managed to say, surprised she could speak at all.

No one had ever asked her before the reasons why she had married Daniel, let alone jumped two steps ahead and come up with the conclusion she must have been protecting someone. Most people, she was sure, had assumed, as Daniel's children had, that she had married Daniel for his money. Until a few moments ago, she had thought Jarrett believed that too..

'You have something to do with me, Abbie,' he replied firmly. 'I want you in my life now, and your past, it seems, is preventing any future for the two of us.'

The only 'future' he had in mind for them was an affair, until his craving for baked Alaska was well and truly satiated!

'We have no future, Jarrett. And the answers to your questions will make no difference to that,' she assured him frostily.

'We'll see,' he returned enigmatically.

She gave a heavy sigh. Jarrett wasn't going to be moved until she had answered his questions. Oh, she knew she could always have Tony escort him from the house, but in the long run what would be the point in doing that? Jarrett was bloody-minded enough just to keep coming back!

She closed her eyes, drawing on the inner strength she had needed so much the last seven years. 'My father worked for Daniel seven years ago,' she began tonelessly. 'He was Daniel's chief accountant.' She didn't look at Jarrett as she spoke, staring down unseeingly at the carpet at her feet. 'My father, very foolishly, decided to—borrow some of Daniel's money for some investments of his own.' She paused. 'Daniel found out about it.'

'I see,' Jarrett said slowly.

'My father wasn't a bad man.' She quickly defended him, sitting forward in her chair.

Jarrett nodded, his expression bland. 'Just very foolish, as you've already said. And men like Daniel Sutherland do not suffer fools gladly!'

'No,' she acknowledged shakily.

'So what was the deal?' Jarrett probed. 'Marriage to him in exchange for not prosecuting your father?'

That was exactly the deal Daniel had offered her! She had been absolutely horrified, both by her father's embezzlement and Daniel's outrageous solution to the problem.

She'd barely known the man her father worked for, had only met him a couple of times before when she'd accompanied her father to a couple of staff occasions after the death of her mother. But Daniel had been a collector of beautiful things, and he'd wanted Abbie to complete his collection…!

'You didn't have to marry him, Abbie,' Jarrett rasped harshly. 'Your father was an adult, responsible for his own actions. You shouldn't have been the one who paid for them.'

'My father was ill, Jarrett,' she told him flatly.

'In fact, he was dying. And I couldn't let him die in a prison cell.'

Daniel had been absolutely clear about her options; marry him, and he would allow his father-in-law to retire gracefully, without a slur to his name, or alternatively he could bring a prosecution and her father would spend his last years in prison.

Abbie didn't even have to concentrate to call into focus that fateful meeting with Daniel in his office seven years ago, or the smug expression on his face as he assured her he intended it to be a proper marriage, that he had been a widower for many years, certainly hadn't been celibate during those years, and had no intention of becoming so with such a beautiful second wife.

He had actually been a very attractive man, tall and slender, with thick iron-grey hair, hard-chiselled features, and an all-year suntan. Yet he'd made Abbie's flesh creep.

That hadn't changed after she married him. In fact, it had got worse, so that each night in his bed his lips and hands on her body had become a nightmare!

'My father died of cancer four years after I married Daniel,' she continued evenly. 'My only consolation is that a year later Daniel died in the same way,' she added hardly, her eyes glittering deeply violet.

'No doubt with you loyally at his side,' Jarrett bit out abruptly.

She shook her head. Playing the role of the grieving widow had been as impossible to her as playing the loving wife! 'Charlie wasn't well at the time, she had German measles, and I—I stayed at home to be with her.'

Cathy had been the one who'd come back to the

house, screaming hysterically that her father was dead, and that no doubt Abbie was happy now!

It had been so long since Abbie was happy, she had forgotten what it felt like. But, for all Daniel's death had released her from her loveless marriage, she still couldn't rejoice in that freedom at the price of another person's death.

Jarrett nodded, eyes narrowed to tawny slits. 'Charlie is, of course, the reason you didn't leave Sutherland after your father's death.'

Abbie gave him a startled look. 'How do you know all this?' she said incredulously. If she left, Daniel had told her, Charlie would remain with him. Again, it had seemed, her options were severely limited.

Jarrett's mouth tightened. 'My mother used the same emotional blackmail on my father for years. Fine, he could divorce her for her infidelities, but if he did she would fight tooth and nail for us! Ironic, really,' he added harshly, 'because when she did finally leave, when my father was in financial ruin, she left us all behind!' He shook his head. 'A man like Daniel Sutherland would never have let you take his daughter away from him.'

'No,' she conceded shakily, vividly remembering that scene with Daniel after her father died. He could no longer hold Abbie through her father, but Charlie was his daughter too, and he would never let Abbie take her away from him.

Abbie had been taught only too well how loving someone gave other people power over you, first with her father, and then with Charlie. She had vowed never to love anyone other than Charlie. Ever!

'That's all over now, Abbie—'

'Is it all over for you, Jarrett?' she challenged him. 'I

don't see you in love, happily married, with children of your own!'

He glowered darkly. 'We weren't talking about me—'

'Of course we were,' Abbie insisted. 'We're both damaged people.'

'Then maybe we can help each other—'

'I don't think so.' She stood up, too agitated by what they had just been talking about to sit down any longer.

'Abbie, you're twenty-seven—'

'And you're thirty-seven,' she replied. 'Come and talk to me again in ten years!'

'You're being ridiculous now—'

'I'm being ridiculous? Oh, Jarrett.' She shook her head pityingly. 'This is my world—'

'It doesn't have to be.' He stood up too. 'Abbie, the life you have now is how you chose to create it. You could just as easily undo it and start again.'

'Do you have any idea how long it's taken me to feel even this secure? Oh, no, Jarrett, my life is staying exactly as it is.'

'Then let me into it.' He lightly grasped her arms. 'Let me in, Abbie,' he persuaded tenderly.

'So that when you choose to leave it's all left in a shambles once again?' She shook her head. 'I don't think so, thank you, Jarrett.'

'What if I don't leave?'

'What if there really are men on the moon?' she returned sarcastically.

He gave an exasperated sigh. 'We don't know for certain that there aren't! Just as you'll never know about me if you don't give us a try.'

She had already told this man too much about herself, let him in too much. 'No, Jarrett,' she told him firmly.

He released her abruptly. 'I think you're wrong, Abbie,' he said flatly. 'Very wrong. I can also see that at the moment you aren't going to budge on this. But if you should change your mind...' He took a card out of the breast pocket of his jacket, writing on the back of it. 'This is my business card, but I've also written my home telephone number on the back of it. Please use it some time.' He continued to look at her for several moments, and, when he received no reply, quietly left.

Abbie remained perfectly controlled until Jarrett had left the sitting-room, but then the tears began to fall. For Jarrett. For herself. For the fact that, with Jarrett's departure, she knew he had not only entered her life, but her heart.

She was in love with Jarrett Hunter. But he had just walked out of her life.

Hell. This had to be what it was like. She had thought hell was being married to Daniel, and not loving him; now she knew it was being in love with Jarrett, and not being with him.

It had been a week since he had left so suddenly. A week when she had picked up the card he had left with her a dozen times, and never once called the telephone number he had written on the back of it. Now she didn't even need to pick up the card; she knew the telephone number off by heart. And still she couldn't call it...

She was terrified! Of loving. Of losing. Daniel's death had been in the form of a release for her, but to be briefly in Jarrett's life, and then be expected simply to walk away when he had taken his fill of her, would be unbearable.

More unbearable than the way she was living now?

She didn't honestly believe it could be. Nothing could be quite as bad as resisting being with the man she loved, and who obviously wanted her in return!

And this afternoon she was to see him again. On business, of course. This afternoon they would sign the contract that would legally pass Sutherland Hotels over to Hunter's.

Abbie had never felt this nervous about a business meeting. Not only did she have to meet Cathy and Danny again—the first time she would have seen both of them together since shortly after Daniel's death—but she also had to face Jarrett. With the full knowledge open between them now of her terrible marriage, and the reason for it. No one else had ever known as much about her as Jarrett did!

Her emotions were in turmoil; she felt elation at the prospect of seeing him again, but anxiety too, because she had never really been in his company knowing that she loved him. She had never been near any man that she loved!

She had dressed with great care this morning; her suit was very businesslike, with its short fitted jacket and just-above-knee-length skirt, but its bright red colour took away any severity of style, and the cream silk blouse she wore beneath the jacket was of fine silk, moulding to the curves of her body. Her hair was plaited loosely down her spine, her make-up light, although her lip-gloss was the same bright red of her suit. Vibrantly alive was how she had looked in the mirror before she'd left for the office this morning, a sparkle of anticipation in the violet-blue of her eyes.

The lawyers were shown into the boardroom first— her own, Cathy and Danny's, and finally the one representing Hunter's. With their arrival Abbie's tension grew. Any minute now she would see Jarrett again...!

Cathy and Danny arrived next, Cathy beautiful in black and white, Danny fashionably dressed in a designer-label suit. A younger version of his father to look at, he hadn't inherited any of the older man's steel. That particular hardness had been inherited by Cathy, apparent now in the calculation of her expression as she and Abbie silently eyed each other across the width of the wide table.

'How's Charlie?' Danny asked pleasantly.

Abbie knew, despite the heartache that had been caused to her after Daniel's death, that Danny's interest in his young half-sister was genuine, that he really was quite fond of Charlie. He was weak, and easily swayed, and it had been his much stronger older sister who had been behind the move to take Charlie from Abbie.

Nevertheless, Abbie felt no lasting warmth towards Danny, aware that he would have sided with Cathy if the move to take Charlie from her had been successful. Abbie didn't think there could be very many mothers who would ever forgive such a terrible deed—she certainly wasn't one of them!

'Well, thank you.' She curtly answered Danny's question, turning away, discouraging any further conversation between the two of them.

The minutes ticked by as they waited for Jarrett's arrival, and Abbie visibly jumped in her seat when the door opened and her secretary announced his arrival, her nerves tensed to the point of breaking as she gazed wide-eyed at the open doorway.

Jonathan Hunter strolled into the room, wearing his own beautifully cut suit with the same elegance as Danny, and yet at the same time exuding a power the younger man could never hope to attain.

Jonathan!

Abbie couldn't help her instinctive glance behind him, searching for Jarrett. But, as the secretary closed the door behind Jonathan, it became glaringly obvious that he was alone. Where was Jarrett? She had built herself up for this meeting, for seeing him today, had been counting on at least being able to look at him. He—

'I'm afraid I have to apologise for my older brother.' Jonathan spoke smoothly as he sat in the chair next to Abbie's before placing his briefcase on top of the long table. 'I'm afraid he's indisposed. However,' he added briskly, 'I do have full power to complete this deal, so that shouldn't pose any problem for us.'

Abbie sat unmoving. What did he mean, Jarrett was 'indisposed'? Was he ill? If so, what was wrong with him?

But the opportunity to question Jonathan on that certainly didn't arise in the next forty-five minutes, at the end of which Sutherland Hotels had changed hands for a vast amount of Hunter money.

It was strange, really; after clinging onto the hotels for the last year, desperately trying to find ways to make them viable, determined not to lose them, Abbie couldn't wait to get the business out of the way so that she might be alone with Jonathan and question him about Jarrett.

But finally the meeting was over, the contracts duly signed, not a word spoken between Abbie and her joint shareholders since Danny's initial query about Charlie. Abbie had nothing to say to either of the Sutherlands. In fact, at this moment, she couldn't help wishing she had just sold off all the Sutherland interests, so that she never had to bother herself with any of it ever again!

How different were her emotions from even a week ago. Sutherland assets, protecting Charlie's interest in them, had been what had kept her going the last two years—and now she just wanted to be rid of them...

'Jonathan.' She stopped him as he would have left

with the others at the end of the meeting. 'Could I have a brief word with you?' she requested awkwardly.

He waited until the last of the lawyers had filed out of the room before answering her impatiently. 'What is it, Abbie?'

There was a coolness to his voice and manner that had never been there before, his usual lazy charm completely absent, causing Abbie to look at him with puzzled eyes. 'Where is Jarrett?' she asked slowly.

He made no move to leave, but neither did he close the door that had been left open for him to depart. 'Why do you want to know?' he asked.

She shrugged. 'I thought it a little—unusual that he wasn't present today.'

'It's all legal, I can assure you, Abbie,' Jonathan replied. 'I'm empowered to—'

'That isn't what I'm talking about, and you know it!' she cut in. 'Shut the door, Jonathan—please!—and talk to me!'

He did shut the door, but those golden eyes so like Jarrett's remained flinty. 'What do you want, Abbie?' he bit out. 'Will it give you some sort of thrill to know you've brought my brother to his knees? To know that he isn't here today because he looks so damned awful you couldn't fail to know what you've done to him?' he accused forcefully. 'Because if it would—'

'I only want to know those things if it's the truth, Jonathan.' She quietly interrupted his tirade.

'Why?' he challenged.

She swallowed hard. She could, as Jarrett had already told her, stay safe in her ivory tower, or she could join the real world. Yes, she might know the pain of loving and losing someone, but if what Jonathan was saying was true, then she could also know the joy of being loved, if only for a short time. Jarrett was afraid of love too, but if he really was in the state Jonathan described, then it was too late for both of them: they were in love with each other!

She took her courage in both hands. 'Have you taken a good look at me today, Jonathan?' she encouraged softly.

He frowned. 'What?'

'Look at me,' she encouraged again. 'Do you see the hollows beneath my eyes? The gauntness of my cheeks? The fact that this suit is a little too big for me, when two weeks ago it fitted me perfectly? Look at me closely, Jonathan,' she repeated emotionally. 'And you'll see a woman brought to her knees!' She met his gaze steadily, her eyes deep pools of emotion.

'My God...!' he breathed. 'You're in love with Jarrett.'

She paused, about to make the hardest confession she had ever made in her life. 'Yes!' The word came out as a relieved sigh. She had said it. Admitted it. She loved Jarrett!

'Then why the hell are you doing this to each other?' Jonathan said exasperatedly. 'No—don't tell me; let me guess. My brother offered you less than love. And you— well, you...' He looked at her consideringly. 'You would have run away from any declaration of love on his part, anyway. A fellow cynic,' he explained as her eyes widened questioningly. 'I have the same mother and father as Jarrett, Abbie,' he reminded her. 'Jarrett bore the brunt of responsibility after my mother left, but I still grew up with my mother's—indiscretions, and my father's dogmatic acceptance of them. We've all avoided love like the plague, but I hope to God that when—or if—love ever comes my way I'll have the courage to accept it, and not destroy myself by trying to deny it. Like the two of you are doing!'

Abbie gave the ghost of a smile. 'It isn't easy, Jonathan.'

'Hell, I know that,' he accepted. 'Try saying it,' he insisted.

She hesitated. Admitting it to herself was one thing...! 'I—I love Jarrett.' She said the words quickly.

'Again,' Jonathan prompted.

'I love Jarrett!' she claimed, more firmly this time.

'Right—now tell him that.' Jonathan took hold of her shoulders and turned her to face the door.

At which point she found herself face to face with Jarrett!

How long had he been there?

Had he heard her shaky confessions of love?

Had Jonathan known Jarrett was standing behind her when he'd encouraged her to say those words?

She turned back to him accusingly, receiving a rueful shrug of apology. He had known his brother had quietly entered the room as the two of them talked. Which meant Jarrett had heard her say she loved him...

Jarrett smiled warmly as she turned back to him. 'I love you, too, Abbie,' he told her throatily.

'My cue to leave, I think,' Jonathan muttered, moving around the two of them to the door. 'Unless you would like me to stay—'

'Go, Jonathan,' Jarrett instructed dryly, his gaze fixed on Abbie's face.

'Just one thing...' Jonathan paused again. 'Can I be best man?'

Jarrett quirked dark brows at her. 'Can he?'

Best man...? That meant a wedding... Did Jarrett want to marry her, after all he had said? After all—?

'You and Jordan can fight it out between yourselves.' Jarrett answered for her. 'Whichever one of you loses can give the bride away. Is that okay with you?' he prompted Abbie gently.

She didn't have anyone else who could do that for her. But marriage...?

'In that case,' Jonathan said before she could find her voice, 'consider me the loser; I would love to give the bride away!'

'Fine. Now just go, hmm?' Jarrett instructed impatiently.

Jonathan's departure left an awkward silence. Abbie felt suddenly very shy as she looked at Jarrett. But Jonathan was right about the way Jarrett looked: he was gaunt and strained.

And yet for some reason he had chosen to come here today, after all...

'I couldn't stay away, Abbie.' Jarrett seemed to guess her thoughts. 'I asked Jonathan to deal with this, but then I just sat at my desk, unable to work. You didn't telephone me, Abbie,' he chided.

No, and if she thought she had suffered this last week because of her silence, then she could see that Jarrett had felt the same pain. She had told him they were two damaged people, and perhaps they were, but they had fallen in love with each other anyway, so perhaps together they might become whole again?

'I wanted to,' she told him as she slowly walked towards him. 'I wanted to so much, Jarrett.' She stood in front of him now, looking straight into those beautiful golden eyes. 'I—' She moistened her lips. 'I was frightened, Jarrett,' she admitted emotionally.

'And you think I'm not?' he teased gently. 'I love you, Abbie, and that's an emotion I never thought I would feel for any woman. But it's all there, Abbie—the need to protect and care, the desire. I never felt there was anything missing from my life before. But without you in it it's colourless and dull, without any sense of purpose, each day just something I have to get through.'

She knew exactly what he meant. She had Charlie, but it wasn't enough for her any more, either. She wanted this man in her life. Needed him. Loved him.

'Do you think we can make it work, Jarrett?'' Her eyes were huge in the paleness of her face. 'Do you think the two of us can forget all the past pain and disillusionment, and just love each other?'

'I think, Abbie, that we can give it a damn good try!' he said determinedly as his arms moved about her.

'A constant diet of baked Alaska?' she said playfully as her arms curved about his waist.

'You are everything I could ever want, Abbie,' he told her intensely. 'Everything!'

And he meant it. She could see that in his face, in the fierce intensity of his gaze. She knew in that moment of truth that Jarrett would love her but never stifle her. What more could she ask from the man she loved so completely?

'Will you marry me, Jarrett?' she asked, almost choked with emotion.

His arms tightened about her. 'I thought you would never ask!' he breathed, before his lips came down gently on hers.

CHAPTER FOURTEEN

JARRETT looked tenderly at the woman cradled so trustingly in his arms, her dark hair splayed out across his chest and the pillow beside him.

Abbie.

His wife.

How he loved calling her that!

They had been married for a week now, a week of absolute happiness, a week when he'd wondered how he had ever lived his life without her in it. He adored her, all of her, her laughter, her caring, her loving, every beautiful inch of her perfection, from her dark shining hair to the tips of her toes.

He didn't doubt for a moment that she loved him in the same way, had known from their very first night together, when she had responded to his caresses, given her own love so beautifully, every moment of unhappiness they had ever known wiped from their lives during that night of love. And what they had, what they shared together, was too precious for either of them to ever want to lose it.

Sometimes he woke like this, in the early hours before dawn, just so that he could lie and watch her sleeping. She was always nestled against him this way, like a contented cat, a smile curving her lips. He meant to make sure she always stayed as happy as she had been this last week. In fact, he intended making it a lifetime's ambition!

* * *

Jarrett was awake beside her, Abbie knew he was, was attuned to his every movement, even the slight change of his breathing when he was awake rather than asleep.

She could hardly believe how happy she was, hadn't known euphoria like this existed. It was because she knew herself well and truly loved, as much as she loved in return.

Jarrett had wasted no time in arranging their wedding after their declarations of love for each other, and they'd been married barely a month later. Jonathan had given her away, Jordan had been Jarrett's best man, and Alison and Charlie had been her attendants. Stephen had just sat through the service with a smug smile on his face; whether that was because he had been the one to introduce the two of them, or because Alison was pregnant, Abbie hadn't been quite sure, but she'd been so happy herself that she'd just returned his smile.

Charlie was thrilled with her new daddy; she barely remembered her own father, and, as she had adored Jarrett from the first, had taken his permanent arrival into their lives as a perfectly natural turn of events.

Their wedding night had been a revelation to Abbie, Jarrett giving pleasure rather than taking it, but revelling in her caresses too as she shyly responded in a way that had totally surprised her. And their lovemaking had only got better, so much so that they were reluctant to leave each other's arms.

'What are you thinking about?' Jarrett murmured softly, those golden eyes warm and loving as Abbie looked up at him.

She wasn't surprised he had realised her own wakefulness; they were so perfectly attuned to each other now. She stretched contentedly, letting her hand rest intimately against his thigh. 'Actually, I was wondering

what you thought of the "paper-bag job" now?' she
whispered mischievously.

Jarrett moved quickly, flipping her over onto her back
as he leant over her. 'You're never going to let me forget
that, are you?' he chuckled.

She grinned up at him. 'Well?' she challenged, moving sensuously against him.

'I'm thinking,' he said, 'that you need to be thor-
oughly loved, Mrs Hunter.'

Mrs Hunter... How she loved the sound of that! 'And
I'm thinking, Mr Hunter,' she whispered again, her arm
moving up about his neck as she pulled his head slowly
down to hers, 'that sounds like an excellent idea!'

'I'm all for excellent ideas,' Jarrett groaned as his
mouth claimed hers in passionate response.

She was 'all for' loving Jarrett for a lifetime. And
longer...

Harlequin is proud to introduce:

HEART OF THE WEST

…Where Every Man Has His Price!

Lost Springs Ranch was famous for turning young
mavericks into good men. Word that the ranch was in
financial trouble sent a herd of loyal bachelors
stampeding back to Wyoming to put themselves on the
auction block.

This is a brand-new 12-book continuity,
which includes some of Harlequin's
most talented authors.

Don't miss the first book,
Husband for Hire by Susan Wiggs.
It will be at your favorite retail outlet in July 1999.

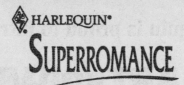

Coming Next Month

HARLEQUIN PRESENTS®

THE BEST HAS JUST GOTTEN BETTER!

#2043 TO BE A HUSBAND Carole Mortimer
Bachelor Brothers
It's the first time for Jonathan that any woman has resisted his charm. What does he have to do to win over the cool, elegant Gaye Royal? Propose marriage? But being a husband is the last thing Jonathan has in mind....

#2044 THE WEDDING-NIGHT AFFAIR Miranda Lee
Society Weddings
As a top wedding coordinator, Fiona was now organizing her ex-husband's marriage. But Philip wasn't about to let their passionate past rest. Then Fiona realized that Philip's bride-to-be didn't love him...but Fiona still did!

#2045 MORE THAN A MISTRESS Sandra Marton
The Barons
When Alexandra Thorpe won the eligible Travis Baron for the weekend, she didn't claim her prize. Travis is intrigued to discover why the cool blond beauty had staked hundreds of dollars on him and then just walked away....

#2046 HOT SURRENDER Charlotte Lamb
Zoe was enraged by Connel's barefaced cheek! But he had the monopoly on sex appeal, and her feelings had become so intense that Zoe couldn't handle him in her life. But Connel always got what he wanted: her hot surrender!

#2047 THE BRIDE'S SECRET Helen Brooks
Two years ago, Marianne had left her fiancé, Hudson de Sance, in order to protect him from a blackmailer. But what would happen now Hudson had found her again, and was still determined to marry her?

#2048 THE BABY VERDICT Cathy Williams
Jessica was flattered when Bruno Carr wanted her as his new secretary. She hadn't bargained on falling for him—or finding herself pregnant with his child. Bruno had only one solution: marriage!